I0761692

MADELAINE BEFORE THE DAWN

ALSO BY

SANDRINE COLLETTE

Nothing but Dust
Just After the Wave
The Forests

Sandrine Collette

MADELAINE BEFORE THE DAWN

Translated from the French by Alison Anderson

Europa Editions
27 Union Square West, Suite 302
New York NY 10003
www.europaeditions.com
info@europaeditions.com

First publication 2026 by Europa Editions

Translation by Alison Anderson
Original title: *Madelaine avant l'aube*

Library of Congress Cataloging in Publication Data is available
ISBN 979-8-88966-172-6

Collette, Sandrine
Madelaine Before the Dawn

Cover design and illustration by Ginevra Rapisardi

Prepress by Grafica Punto Print – Rome

Printed in Canada

CONTENTS

Qui es in caelis

MADELAINE BEFORE THE DAWN

Prologue

The earth trembles to their heavy step. They are hurrying, with the almost hypnotic slowness of large bodies exhausted after a day's labor—now interrupted well ahead of time, when the boy came.

They are walking side by side, the man and the horse, both stinking of sweat that has dried on rough skin. The man wipes the dust that is turning gray on his brow, and the horse shakes its head to get rid of the flies. The boy is walking ahead, and turns around to wait for them. He doesn't say anything, but everything about his attitude shows his impatience. He wants them to hurry, for the man they call Eugène-le-Fort to be as quick as the wind. He wants the powerful horse to lunge forward and carry them on its back because up there, Aelis—or was it Ambre? he's not sure—told him again and again, in a leaden voice: *Go quick. Tell him it's serious.*

And the child ran fit to burst his lungs. At the edge of the river he hailed the ferrywoman with cries like roars, he fidgeted on the ferry, then set off at a run again the minute his foot felt the shore. He went through the woods, met a few men bent over their fields, who pointed the way with weary arms; he searched the edge of the dark forest for the sight of the imposing golden horse, and only stopped when he was standing by its hooves. There he delivered his urgent message and Eugène immediately set about unhitching the animal from its shafts, abandoning the tree trunk they were hauling in the middle of a clearing. The boy thought then that they would return the way the mistress of the house had said—quickly, very quickly. And yet the two creatures following him are making their way with heavy steps, taking long, drowsy, endless strides, the weight of the day allowing nothing better for man and horse, that's just how it is. In his heart, however, Eugène is shouting that he's on his way, shouting for them to wait.

He doesn't know why the boy came, the boy gave no explanation, only that Aelis—or was it Ambre?—weeping, sent him with a forceful command, Go quick, woe is upon us. And the man Eugène with his long slow steps paced to the horse's, is heading toward that woe. Shaking, his first reaction had been to grab the boy by the shoulder. *My sons?* The boy looked at him, not understanding, and Eugène got a hold of himself, at this time of day his sons are working in the fields, on their land as tenant farmers—his sons are not at home.

On the shore of the river The Crone is waiting for them, the boy had warned her he'd be back before long. She had maneuvered the barge to a place where the horse could embark. Jéricho weighs eight hundred kilos and the small craft tilts when he steps on board, without hesitating; despite the fact that The Crone has been ferrying him across every morning and every evening for half the year the last eight years, she says, once again, as she turns to Eugène, Keep him still. Eugène doesn't reply, he never replies. The Crone's words are just routine. With a hand on the horse's neck he observes the old woman as she hauls the boat along the cable, fist over fist, all her nerves turning her face and scrawny arms blue with effort, and he thinks, too, as he has done every morning and every evening for half the year for eight years, that it's madness to leave the ferry to this woman. That she's too old for it. Everyone whispers about it. Everyone agrees that the cable will hold the ferry, come what may, but that she, The Crone, will end up dead, tugging the way she does with her muscles, with the veins drawing winding swollen paths across her gray temples, and those croaking sounds she emits with each tug of her arms, one after the other, her palms scorched by the rope. Everyone talks about it and no one does a thing, that's the way it will be as long as there's no accident. It suits them for the old woman to run the ferry, since there's no bridge anymore. Eugène remembers the bridge. It was destroyed when he was ten or twelve years old, and they're keen, the folk of La Foye, not to rebuild it. He can't recall why: that's the way it is, is all—the way it is, and then to be protected from the world.

But it's taking so long, he thinks, clenching his fists to keep from grabbing the cable in The Crone's place. Such a little river.

And so he closes his eyes and since this is his habit, he tries to take some rest during the few minutes of the crossing. The weight of the day is crushing his back. Too much exhaustion, but that's normal. It's always like this. Every day. Exhaustion is life. And he tells himself that he no longer feels it, he's made it his own, in this huge body that other folk assume is protected from wretchedness and stumbling. Eugène stands in the middle of the ferry, his gaunt features drawn with fatigue, his shoulders tense, his hands as wide as a bear's paw, capable of seizing any tool or any work. Legs slightly apart, not to slip, not to worry Jéricho standing next to him. He is alone on the barge. He's always alone. No one wants to cross the Basilic. The long green river beneath his feet writhes through the land like the deadly little snake it is named after. But Eugène knows: the Basilic is not a river for snakes. Its near-emerald color does not come from the scales of reptiles hidden by the thousands in its recesses, as those who like to pretend they're afraid would assert. It is a river of rock and freshwater algae.

Eugène opens his eyes. The shore is approaching, he can feel it from the motion of the ferry. The boy is leaning forward, ready to spring, when The Crone grabs him by the arm and shoves him back. She's seen too many little boys drown from their impatience, slipping under the hull before anyone has time to save them. She maneuvers the craft and soon they are brushing against the reeds. Jéricho is already stepping over the gunwale. The world that had briefly come to a halt continues on its way. Eugène places one hand on his heart, it is beating hard. It's impossible to see from here because of the forests; the farm is to the northeast, almost one league away. Too far to arrive quickly and too near to prepare himself for what he is about to find. For a few seconds he falters. He will either have to run, or to go away in the opposite direction; he feels incapable of either.

So he heads off behind the boy who, when he sees him on the path, runs far ahead to reach his own home; before long Eugène can no longer see him at all. They walk, the horse and the man, and fear drains his mind. He can think of nothing but the moment when he will arrive at the top of the rise, behind which stands the house—that hill which gave its name to the three little farms that are set there: The Rises. He wonders what is happening there, what it is he doesn't know yet. Aelis must be alive, if she sent the boy, but Aelis doesn't matter, what matters is all the rest, and the boy didn't talk about the rest, walled up in terrified silence as he was, and for that reason Eugène can do nothing but tremble.

And it is long, that league under a sun that does not want to set, and it is short, it is basically just as Eugène has imagined it: a slow and terrible walk toward the darkness, and until the end he hopes he is mistaken, that the boy is mistaken, that Aelis too is mistaken, he hopes that the day has not come, the day he has dreaded ever since Madelaine arrived. He prays for it to be no more than a dream, or a mistake.

Because when Eugène first finds himself far enough along to see the scene unfolding there, which means near his home, he doesn't understand; but the moment he can see the strange bodies and the dogs straining toward him, howling, enraged by violence and blood, he knows that nothing will ever be the same. He knows that he will lose everything that day, that all he will have left will be his eyes to weep, he knows that the order of things has been shattered once again and that no one will be able to efface it or go back, it will erase in a few moments what he has spent half his life building, and his life no more than a wisp of straw. In a curious torpor he has time to gaze at the dust the wind has set spinning, and he himself is one of those specks of dust. Then he hears the women's cries when they see him coming, and this reality radiates all the way to him and he feels that now he must be quick.

One

I'm in the doorway next to Rose and we're listening to the dogs bark. Actually, we're not really listening to their howling; it's a faint noise from beyond, in the distance, but not very far, and it's been annoying the mongrels like this for days, four or five days, and we can't find that noise. It's not all the time, just now and then, at sunset, when the coming dark troubles our vision. There are shadows, furtive movements, maybe in our imagination, except that—

The dogs are howling.

We're in the habit of being vigilant. In the habit of listening. This world offers no promises or certainties, other than the fact we will die, too soon no doubt, our lives are short, brutal, exhausting. But like Eugène says, that's normal. It's the life our parents led, and their parents before them.

A world that doesn't change.

As for us in all that, at the end of the farthest lands, we're unchanging, like the ancient forests that surround us. We could be characters in the old tales the storytellers have been peddling forever, with one simple difference: here, the tales don't end well. Kings never come to abduct one of our shepherdesses, or if they do come, it's to rape her, not to make her a queen.

Well, anyway, here we are, and there's this thing in the air that annoys us every evening and we don't know what it is. So we keep watch. My hearing is better than Rose's. Rose has some years behind her. It's not so much the number of years as the number of sorrows: because the sorrows add up much more quickly and are much stronger than the years. I'm not saying she's well and truly old, but she doesn't hear as well as she used to. Some afternoons she no longer hears the sound of my steps when I come in at the back of the house, over the wooden threshold that's so worn it no longer creaks. And I realize she sees me at the last minute, her gaze is startled. But she's impassive. Just that blue time-faded iris that is like a slap a bolt of lightning and then it recedes again beneath her heavy lids. Rose goes on chopping the vegetables or slicing the bread, I hear her murmur, Oh, it's you. Anyone other than me, and that's the point, would ignore the tiny pause in her gesture, the hesitation when I come in through the door that's always open and doesn't make a sound either: my presence has caught her off guard. She's scratching her ear. These damned wax plugs, she mutters. But I know it's not wax. It's age. We pretend, she and I, that nothing has happened. Rose mustn't get old. Old people don't last in this place, they're not wanted, they can't.

Rose lives alone in her little house. At one point she had two sons and they left. There are not many who have left the Hinterland but those two did, and they never came back. In the beginning they sent news, with tradesmen who came this far and would recite a message. The sons said it was better where they were, but they didn't suggest she join them. Rose was a little ruffled, and then she put it aside—anyway, she couldn't imagine leaving her little patch of earth. Little by little their messages stopped coming, that's the way men are, she said. Out of sight out of mind. She hasn't seen them in twenty years. I think it's sad, especially when I notice a handful of things still folded on the beds, and despite the years a little of their buried smell lingering deep in the fabric. Rose says you mustn't be sorrowful, we mustn't waste our strength on questions that are too big for us, words I can't retain. I'm nothing to her, nothing in the way of a blood relation, I'm here, that's all, she took me in one day when I was little and dying of hunger on the road, and I stayed. That was eight years ago.

Her sons' absence settled in slowly, Rose is used to it, like when you lose a dog: the first few days you can still hear him, you think he'll suddenly be there by your feet with his sweet doggy face and his eyes straining while you're filling his bowl. After some time has gone by, a week or two or more, you stop listening for the sounds of his presence. And later still you forget there ever was a dog in the house. For Rose it's the same with her sons. It took longer than with an animal and yet it's the same thing, it began to blur in her memory, she stopped waiting for them. Rose gets angry if you put it to her like that but I think it happened gently. Except that absence is never gentle. It's just time. That's how it is. You may not agree, but time consumes everything, good things and bad. It's nibbled away at sorrow, it's nibbled away at absence.

But I'm here and I won't leave. The difference with Rose's sons is that they dreamt of traveling; with me, I ended my traveling here. When she's in a bad mood she reproaches me for staying, saying it's simply because she feeds me. There is truth in that. It's a miracle to eat every day and it's also because I love Rose that I'm here. And then this country, bitter and harsh, it speaks to me, it resonates, even if deep down we are its prisoners, a spit of land cut off from others by the river, and no one has fought us for it. We don't have the right to leave, there are rules. We belong to the Ambroisies. I go along with all of that. It's our world and it is wild, right down to the glow in the children's eyes when it's bread day and the stirring smell of baking dough floats above the village.

Anyway, it's been going on for too long, those dogs barking at nightfall, and Rose thinks it's coming from up there. From Eugène's place, or Léon's, she isn't sure, the farms are too close together. It's not nasty barking, we know those dogs. It's rather as if something were poking its way toward the dogs and exciting them, we can't hear them growling from the back of their throats, the way they do when there's a real problem and their hackles are raised. But it's making Rose frown. She looks at me and says suddenly, astonished, A curious lad like you, and you didn't go nose around up there? I turn my head the other way, it means no. I don't want her to know that I did go up there and saw nothing. There's just that smell, only I must be mistaken, the smells in the barn mingle together, human, animal, and then the hay and earth. There's time enough, because I'm bound to figure out what's lurking around our nights, we can't allow things to happen without being sure what it is, whether it's a threat. The only sensation I have at the moment is contradictory: it's not dangerous but there is danger. It means no harm, otherwise the dogs' barking would be full of alarm and rage. If we left it at that, it would be out of laziness, and we're not lazy. As I said, we are vigilant. So there's something going on up there and I'm going to find out what it is.

We live at the end of the earth. The river Basilic winds along the entire border of our region, cutting it off from the rest of the universe. On our side of the river, there are a few swamps, then further back, the village, and behind the village, scattered farms like Rose's, which belongs to the group of three houses called The Rises. There are forests and there are fields and further still, it all spreads out and ends at an almost vertical mountain of lava that no one has ever ventured to climb.

The Basilic, we don't know where it ends. Those who left the country headed straight and none of them ever came back to tell us. I don't know anyone who has walked along the river to the end. From time to time I go and sit on the riverbank. I gaze at the color of the water and I think it's beautiful. On days of blue weather the tall trees are reflected on its surface and it's an explosion of green, brown, and yellow. But what's most special about our river, more than its color and its mirrors and the giant trout that live there, is that there are no bridges for crossing it. That's why this is the end of the earth. Way back in time there was a bridge. It was destroyed long before I arrived, I remember that, I swam across the Basilic, and I almost drowned.

But there is a ferrywoman. We don't really know why she's there, other than the fact that Eugène crosses with his horse mornings and evenings half the year to go to haul timber on the other side. But the ferrywoman is there every day, winter, summer, autumn, and spring. I know as much because I often go with Eugène when Rose is still sleeping and I'm bored in the gray dawn. Eugène's farm is set higher up than ours, just across from Ambre and Léon's. Eugène has to walk along the edge of our garden when he goes down to the ferry; on the way to the river I run alongside him, I breathe in the smell of the big golden horse, I look out at the countryside. Then he sends me back to Rose. I'm not allowed to cross the river. When I get back, Rose is up and I hear her calling as I climb the hill—Bran! Bran! I'm here. I run over to her. I pretend not to know that the name she has given me is that of her youngest son, that I'm a sort of ghost, a trace of vanished beings.

Rose is the memory of the village. She's known everyone and she remembers everything. She's a healer and that's why she's been inside all the houses and all the farms, and on rainy evenings she tells me stories about the locals. I don't have a memory like hers but I have instinct. How to explain it: I sense everything. What isn't said, what isn't shown. It's not just that I'm a mischief-maker—Léon's the one who calls me a mischief-maker when I start skulking around too close to his house—it's inside me. And I don't have the words to express it, either, so it doesn't really matter, but that's the way it is, I know everything. I observe and I notice. I intuit. I understand. That's my strength. And then I don't look like much—much in particular, that is. I'm average, in everything, my size, my strength, my intelligence, my meanness. That's why I can go all around and the villagers don't chase me away, they look at me from a distance, they don't say anything, they forget about me. And Rose sticks up for me. In the beginning people spoke badly to me, they even kicked me. So Rose gave a good shout and it stopped. Now I'm part of the scenery, this scenery of deep forests and fields of thick earth, and I feel at home even though I came from beyond the forests and to everyone I'm still a stranger.

Every morning I open my eyes on the Hinterland and I gaze at the huge dark green trees, darker even than the river, with white and blue and purple wildflowers growing the minute a gap in the leaves gorges them with a little sunlight. The soil is rich and black and the gardens produce abundantly when the weather doesn't wreck everything. In summer the orchards are colorful with fruit, and tall stakes support their heavy branches. The crushing heat of the following months comes with terrible storms that drench the ground and furrow the slopes, and we've had no droughts like the ones they had further north. Here it's more about damp and rot than heat. We survive. Just barely. We subsist.

The villagers' grandparents and great-grandparents built small farms of yellow stone, with roofs that embrace the rain and let it slide to the end of their arms. The windows are low as if to keep the light from entering, but it's the frost they're keeping out, with narrow openings and yawning chimneys where you can stand right next to the flames when you come back from a bitter cold day. We dread the stifling heat of summer, too, even if it only lasts a month or two: you have to break the sun's rays, they hit too hard, and all the little windows have thick wooden shutters that are closed during those baking hours, the same as when it's icy cold—well, they're closed most of the time, to be honest. I run outside and breathe in the air and I don't care whether there's drought or frost. The Hinterland flows in my blood, in my veins.

I like The Rises best of all. This tiny hamlet, it's my country all to itself, and Rose and I huddle together halfway up the slope, far enough away from the village to have our peace and quiet, and close enough to Eugène's and Léon's farms, which overlook us, not to feel completely alone. Rose's farm is modest, a rectangle containing one room where everything goes on, with a corner used for a sleeping area back in the days when Rose had a husband and her two sons who left. As soon as the sky allows it, the door is opened onto the outside world, and we cross that border dozens of times a day. The sweet warm air spreads through the house on our heels when we come in, and there's a scent of grass and thyme and mint. All the little farms are alike. Up there, on Eugène and Aelis's farm, everything is like at Léon and Ambre's place, the construction is identical to ours, with the little main building and a barn on the other side of the yard. In the valley the village houses are even smaller, and some even touch, with adjoining walls leaning against each other, but the architecture is the same and the stone, too, the local yellow stone that looks dirty in winter, and has a golden sheen when the sun strikes it.

I've learned to look at this landscape with Eugène, since I go up to wait for him at dawn, and then we come back down, me following in his footsteps as he heads to the river with the big horse. We could swallow this path in one gulp without seeing anything around us, but we break off after a hundred strides, or even less, when we're walking along the farm further down. Ambre is always there at the edge of the yard, she's sweeping, distracted. I know she's got her eye on us, not the dust, even if we're like the dust, too: every day there we are, again.

Ambre is Aelis's sister and Eugène's sister-in-law. Ambre is the unlucky one, because her husband Léon—I'm hunting for the words again and can't find them, maybe because when I see how lovely she is, with her smile to make you faint, I tell myself she didn't deserve that husband of hers, and maybe not talking about him will make him disappear bit by bit. But Léon is alive all right and Ambre is waiting for us, for what are sometimes the only words of the day, the only tenderness, a few seconds at dawn and a few at sunset. I know these moments by heart. There's something so sweet about them that it overwhelms me, and yet for years I've been sitting a bit further away, acting as if I'm not looking at Ambre, not looking at Eugène, and I never get tired of what's vibrating in the air. Oh, yes: Léon, Ambre's husband, is a drunkard and a bastard.

Every one of those mornings, Ambre holds out a handful

of grass for the big horse, and he stops. Eugène stops, too, and so do I, there by his side, and then I step away. Make myself scarce. I fill myself with them. They don't say much, their words are slow, not that they're not in a hurry, but that's the way this country is, folk take their time, you can rest your back, your legs, your arms for just a moment. They don't look at each other, Ambre and Eugène, not really, they're watching the horizon, not so much face to face as side by side, because what connects them opens out before their eyes, this land, here, its tilled fields and dense forests, the sun rising and making warm yellow and orange halos in the sky. They know, although they can't see them, that the villagers below are also getting ready for the day. Twenty or so houses cluster along a stony path flattened over centuries by the hooves of oxen and horses. Ambre and Eugène—with their two little farms on the heights that offer magical views, that on stormy days take the wind full on, remote from the world and yet so close—they live there like recluses, the heirs to the discovery of a natural spring that made it possible to build The Rises. There are several of these lonely houses scattered at the whim of water, and they have more land than the village houses, you don't hear their dogs as much, and they're not as close to each other. These quiet buildings can be found at all four cardinal points, forming a ring of old thatched roofs around the village of La Foye. The people who dwell there don't see much of each other, but they know that they are there.

And as they gaze out at the invisible village, Eugène and Ambre cast furtive glances at each other, too, because it would be too hard afterwards, too hard to walk away. Just to hear each other, sense the other's presence, and these words, always, never said, even though I can feel them running along my spine and trembling at my lips, since I had to stay, thinks Eugène, why did life take this path, if Aelis and Ambre are the same, why did fate deal him the wrong hand, for years the answers have escaped him, that's the way it is, is all.

These moments out of time between Eugène and Ambre . . . even if it's not quite normal, I respect them and I protect them. I'm a butterfly that opens its wings to hide them from the world, the time it takes for a few words and a few smiles, even if they don't need to be hidden, they're doing nothing wrong. I'm the marmot watching over the hill, the eagle gliding above them. I try to put right a wrong that I don't understand and on which I have no purchase, and I'm a helpless witness to that force between them that can't be set free, because that's something that isn't done. Because things have always been this way, and no one can change them: there are entire worlds that cannot be moved.

I'd never seen any before I saw the two of them. Ambre and Aelis are twins. It doesn't happen often, and folk are wary when a mother's womb gives birth twice, one infant right after the other, and they're relieved when one of the two babies dies at birth. Because for them there's nothing normal about bodies and faces that are two peas in a pod all their life long, those creatures you can never tell whether it's the one or the other, whether they're really human, whether deep down they're not the devil. Rose laughed when she told me, a long time ago, that Ambre and Aelis both survived and it caused their parents no end of worry to make room for two children at once, and two girls to boot, who wouldn't be strong like sons, who'd have to be married off, and they'd practically have to pay someone to take them off their hands. What's more, their parents very nearly did throw them into the Basilic one night when all the village was asleep. But the babes were so strikingly beautiful; no doubt their parents decided to keep them out of a sort of confused superstition, a mixture of fascination and fear, they didn't dare undo what heaven had done, if only it was heaven.

As children Aelis and Ambre were inseparable. They didn't have the words then to talk about soulmates, and yet there was no other word, two little girls who were as one, their communion of spirit was that strong, two little girls who followed each other like shadows, each reproducing the other's gestures so exactly, without copying or consulting, right down to the sound of their own voices, until even their own mother could not tell them apart. The two of them created a world unto themselves. They needed no one else, they were mindless of the looks people gave them, either because their resemblance was so astonishing or because their beauty was so fascinating. They made up stories that they alone understood, that they alone could laugh over. Their childhood was a time of sharing and of happiness.

As they grew, the sisters continued to look absolutely alike. I myself, having only known them as adults, have had a lot of trouble finding ways to tell them apart, I'm not sure I always succeed. They're still very pretty. There was no difficulty in finding husbands for them, which was of some consolation to their parents, but for the girls themselves it came as a terrible shock. For the first time, they were being separated. No doubt they'd always believed that would never happen—not that they wouldn't be married, but that they would be taken away from each other. Rose tells the story of how they wept so bitterly that the families agreed to settle them next door to each other at the two farms on The Rises, so they could see each other whenever they wanted. The future bridegrooms, Eugène and Léon, did not object, were only too pleased to have been the favorites, chosen to marry girls who were so beautiful. (But how were they chosen? Neither one really knows: among the elders and friends, back in the days when all of them, Aelis and Ambre and Léon and Eugène, were still children, an old woman must have said one day that that would be a good solution, and the idea was born.) And thus they moved into houses that were almost as identical as their spouses. As far as looks went, what difference was there between Aelis or Ambre? I wouldn't have paid any notice to that, either, I would have said, like Eugène, shrugging his shoulders with a smile: They're the same. What a mistake.

From outside, what Eugène and Léon didn't realize was that it was inside they had to go. From outside, yes, two peas in a pod; but inside? Where Ambre was concerned, there was sweetness and something ravishing; but as for Aelis, bitterness and coldness. It's like the fairytale about two sisters, one who is charming, the other who is mean, except that in the fairytale, the mean girl is ugly, the tale is too obvious. In any event, Eugène made the wrong choice, and it was terribly unfair because Ambre also drew the short straw with Léon, but the way I see it, if you have folk who are mean, or afflicted in some way, you might as well put them together. I hear what they say in the village, how it would've been better to give Aelis to Léon and end up with two unhappy souls instead of four; deep in their hearts, it gladdens them to know that the twins have spread their sorrow; it comforts them in their little gray beliefs.

They didn't always say that, back in the days when Léon worked hard. In his youth they spoke of him as being the best clog-maker the region had ever known, and it was no lie. He took care to finish his work on his customers' feet, shaving smooth the places that rubbed, rounding out corners that didn't suit.

For so long there had been only one kind of wooden clog. A few sizes—children's, women's, men's—with which you simply had to make do, stuffing them with woven straw or burlap, and it was the feet that adapted to the clogs; the clogs never adapted, even when wood is soft, it doesn't turn supple. That was where Léon had been a genius: for a few pennies extra he'd begin widening, hollowing, arranging. He told people to walk back and forth so he could see where their toes were pinched; they felt like gentlemen or ladies, they put on airs. Everyone left with the finest clogs they could hope for; some were cured of old wounds or scars they'd lived with for years without any hope of improvement. In this country people go through three or four pairs a year, it's the best thing they can wear. There were clogs to be made for hundreds of years, time enough for Léon to have a son to take over the workshop, and for the son himself to father another son, and another.

There were clogs with no end in sight, until—

Then there was the accident.

And since then Léon has been dragging his leg the way you drag your sorrow, diminished in his body but more than anything in his soul, because it was his soul that was hit hardest. And there has been nothing for it, in all these years, neither the austere beauty of the land where they live isolated beyond the meanders of the Basilic, nor Ambre's own beauty—with Aelis, she's the loveliest woman in the land. Léon began to drink a few months after his accident and has never stopped. No one really knows the depths of his abyss. Other folk, those in the village, think he didn't simply slip in his workshop, that his head also took a blow, like his leg, which got twisted the wrong way round, and neither his leg nor his head ever really came back.

Wine replaced work, and effaced Ambre. Never again did anyone in the hamlet murmur that they made a fine couple: that's all finished. By the time I arrived, folk were laughing behind their backs, saying Léon should never have married the devil's daughter, he should have turned her down; now it's too late.

It's the end of the afternoon, and I can hear the voices of Eugène's sons, the two eldest; the youngest one still stays at the farm. What they've been doing today I don't know, out looking for wood or berries, taking the pigs to the woodland pasture, sometimes stopping to play with little sticks when no one can see them, because in spite of the work they both do they're still children. They see me from a ways off and call out, waving. *Bran, Bran! Come!* I run toward them. I like Eugène's sons, I like that they're children, how it means they forget the world is a hard place. Every evening we run wildly around the houses until we're in a tangle of limbs, and finally we collapse on the ground, shouting and laughing. Little Mayeul joins us and rolls on top of us, we're careful not to crush him, he's only six. Sometimes we stay there entwined and we look up at the sky and the falling light. We don't speak, the vision of a world that is beyond us and the warmth of our tangled bodies are enough. It's really different from life at Rose's. It does me good, this break.

Me with Eugène's sons.

There should have been five boys, but two of them died. That's normal, we're used to that, too: half the children don't make it past ten years of age. Those who do are the sturdiest ones, it's the law of nature; it is how the race perpetuates itself, with its vigor strengthened and reinforced—though there are spells when it falters, with the accumulation of cold and hunger and illness. These recent years have contributed heavily, taking

Aelis and Eugène's children. What's most disturbing is how, every time, Aelis turned away from her boys—not that she had given up altogether, but she understood, before Eugène did, that it was all pointless, too late, too hard. Birds push their weakest fledglings from the nest, foxes abandon frail or misshapen cubs in the forest. Aelis, like an animal, preserves her strength for the others, the ones who are in with a chance; there, too, Eugène has never understood where it came from, that sort of prescience of hers. Simply, you can't be a child in this life, you have to grow up, and quick.

Germain, the eldest, is ten years old now. He's both thin and robust. I can see the paternal pride in Eugène's gaze whenever Germain comes with us, the pride saying that Germain is already a little Eugène, and that is good, the boy's getting stronger and stronger, leaving the specter of premature death far behind, even though nothing is ever certain. He's so strong, Germain, that I keep well away from him. There's too much blood in him. When he grabs me by the neck to play, it's brutal, he squeezes, he digs his nails in, and I feel myself shrinking, I wish I were a tortoise, I wish I could retreat inside to a place where he can't get to me. Afterwards I go away. I scrap with Artaud or even Mayeul. Their skin is bruised from their older brother's grip.

Germain loves being tired. I sometimes tell myself it's the only thing that might calm him down, he goes after that physical exhaustion, calls out for it. He works relentlessly from morning to night, too hard for a boy his age, he works himself to the bone, and tiredness always makes him laugh. In the beginning Aelis and Eugène thought this was some sort of madness, but it's nothing of the kind. Leaning on his crook, Germain comes back from a long day in the pastures at the edge of the woods, dragging his feet, his voice broken, not even trying to speak. Half asleep already, he eats the little that is allotted to him, swallowing with a laugh, lying down with a laugh, and laughing in his sleep until dawn wakes him and that terrible fire gets him out of bed, his eyes shining with a fever that is no illness. He runs off to work the way a man answers the toll of a bell, instinctively, out of necessity, with a burst of energy. On days when he's not allowed to go to work because wolves have been spotted, or a rumor is going around the village that there are brigands on the other side of the Basilic, Eugène hears him tossing and turning all night long, his body consumed by an untiring violence. On those nights, Germain doesn't laugh, there's a dark gleam in his black eyes that nothing can quell. Eugène falls asleep all the same, vanquished, leaving the boy to his demons, falls asleep to search his innermost depths for such strength, he sometimes envies his son—what he, Eugène, could do if in his heart he had that almost superhuman energy. In the morning, as soon as Aelis has risen, Germain follows her like a shadow, mute, drawn in on himself, a fusion ready to explode. The minute they open the door he leaps up, and both Aelis and Eugène feel as if they are releasing a wild animal. Some of the tension leaves the house. They sigh, the boy's already opening the pen, he brings out the two pigs to lead them to the pasture. On his way he pockets the chunk of bread his mother holds out to him, waves his hand, doesn't turn around. They can hear him laughing when he reaches the edge of the woods, Germain's laugh, later this will become an expression among the villagers, and it will endure, folk will say, Don't you remember? A germain sort of laugh.

Artaud joins his older brother a bit later, he's always a little behind. Artaud, the second-born, is only a year younger. He came quickly, maybe too quickly, as if Germain had grabbed all the strength and there wasn't enough left, not quite, neither strength nor brilliance. Artaud's not sickly or weak, he's just *a bit less*. Less lively, less quick, less solid than his brother, less resistant, less cheerful. Sometimes when I watch him running behind Germain I feel sorry for him. He can never keep up. At some point the older boy stops and lets Artaud catch up, otherwise the race could last forever. Artaud doesn't give in. He tries. He's not to be pitied, because he isn't in pain: his entire being is given over to imitating Germain, for whom he has boundless admiration. His big brother is his passion, his reason for living. The fascination transcends him, he's neither bitter nor sad. And Germain always lavishes encouraging words on his younger brother, and in this way he returns the friendship that makes families what they are, the kind of friendship that never fails, is never found wanting. They walk together shoulder to shoulder, most often herding the pigs, until the day comes when they'll be allowed to help with the real work, in the fields and the woods, and then they'll leave the animals to the younger children or to the village swineherd; for the time being this makes them proud, it makes them feel grown-up. They have their switches in hand, and lately they've been going off for the entire day. Seen from behind they look like a pair of wingless angels. Artaud keeps an eye on the pigs while Germain collects branches. In the afternoon each of them loads a bundle on his back, and bent with the weight they walk behind the piglets. They cast knowing glances at the creatures: one of them will be slaughtered for Christmas, and the other some time in February, when he's fatter. Oh, the joy of those winter months, when there's meat again—they think about it every morning as they take the piglets to fatten them up with acorns, roots, and beechmast.

The only way in which Artaud differs from Germain, something neither one is aware of, is in appearance. Germain has his father's square, regular features, marks of strength and will, but in equal measure, Artaud has inherited his mother's splendid beauty. He shares his brothers' unruly brown hair and dark eyes, but his features are remarkably fine, with large luminous eyes, surpassing in brilliance anything the village has produced in a very long time, surpassing even his own mother and aunt.

The other boys call him a girl. Artaud knows they laugh at him, so he runs over to them, only escaping a thrashing because Germain is right behind, ready to lash out at anyone within reach. The pair of them spin, leap, strike, strangely intoxicated, and Germain's laugh rises in the air, causing the sky to vibrate. They stand back to back so no one can take them by surprise, and Artaud can feel his brother's laugh running along his spine, the world can collapse around them they're together they need no one not even the youngest, their little brother.

Mayeul is the fifth son. Between Artaud and him, two infants died at birth, one after the other, thus enlarging the age gap between the boys. Mayeul is six and still stays at the farm with Aelis, when you're six you're not yet out of the woods, if you ever are. Is that why there's so little tenderness, because you mustn't get too attached to creatures who can die on you all of a sudden, is it because life has exhausted that tenderness, but tenderness doesn't exist either, and Aelis looks after her sons the way she looks after the animals, or Rose looks after me, with care but very little emotion.

But Mayeul has a head and heart full of affection and God knows where he got it from, with no model, no example, it just came like that. He expresses it in a way that overwhelms Aelis: the little boy doesn't stop talking. All day long, from the moment he could make a sound, he has been babbling. He tells stories, comments on the things he sees, on what I'm doing when I'm ferreting around near their place, on what his mother is doing, on the voice that sometimes shouts at him to be quiet. Nothing stops him, not even Aelis's mood when she's having a bad day, the boy keeps on chattering, virtually never pausing for breath, and he babbles in her wake, glued to her skirts, wherever she goes in the house or the yard he's right behind her. More than once I saw Aelis step back when she was hanging up the laundry or picking some vegetables and she knocked the boy over, he was that close. In fact, she does it on purpose, she reaches a point where she can't stand it anymore. She'd rather he would cry. But he gets up, dusts himself off, looks at her apologetically, is it for her sake or his, he hesitates for a moment and if Eugène is home he runs to the stables where the big golden horse is feeding and he curls up in a corner and starts prattling all over again. Jéricho sometimes turns his head toward him, as if asking for a caress. Eugène has to come and get Mayeul for supper, otherwise the little boy would stay there all night. We can't let him live there, says Eugène when Aelis rolls her eyes, and yet it's in the barn they find him whenever he has vanished; at the age of six Mayeul knows how to tell Jéricho what to do, can get his own way—the horse obeys him with good grace but the thing is, a child is not meant to be spending his life in a barn, and although Eugène knows his son goes there for refuge when Aelis has been too strict with him, he still doesn't like it. When she sees them coming back, Aelis bows her head. She's ashamed of what she did, ashamed for rejecting her living child. She knows how lucky she is to have sons. She knows people in the village who've lost all their sons.

She knows people who—

Ambre, in the farm next door, Ambre has no child to raise.

Ambre and Léon's house has never echoed to the crying of an infant. There have been no dead children, no: it simply doesn't take. That's how the villagers put it, in hushed voices, and sometimes the same thought occurs to Aelis, the way they would speak about a ewe or a cow, making little ones comes so easy. It just happens all by itself, it comes more often than they'd like, they don't know how it works, but it works. But don't say that to Ambre. At Ambre's place, there are no children.

Worthy folk draw up their list of possible causes, of course. That drunkard Léon. That twin sister. The gossips laugh behind their hands, saying Léon must not be all that robust, and as for her . . . Must be the devil's work, still. And yet Aelis, her sister, has three fine lads. It makes for plenty of tittle-tattle. It makes for plenty of opinions, hunches, rumors. I've heard bits and pieces but the minute they see me coming, the women fall silent. They don't trust me. Rose might be close behind. Those Rises folk, is what they call us, those Rises folk talk among themselves and Rose has a real soft spot for Ambre. No one wants to mess with her. Rose has a sharp tongue, high and mighty like people who have no fear, her words can be worse than a slap in the face. Folk keep mum around her. And besides, they're in too great a need of her.

Ambre has come to Rose more than once, about the child. Rose has given her simples, infusions; she murmurs secrets in the young woman's ear, but when it won't take, it won't take.

Rose says they're not right for each other, Léon and Ambre. So nature itself is dispirited. Every time—but what is meant by that *every time*, I'd rather not know—so, every time, Ambre goes down to Rose's place, in tears because of the blood that is there again. It moves me and annoys me at the same time, I don't understand why she's weeping about it and yet, when Ambre is there outside the door with her eyes red and puffy, I wish with all my strength I could console her. Rose sends me packing. This is women's business. Stop circling around us, she says. I go outside and breathe the air.

Ambre's sorrow is kept silent, hidden inside; sterile flesh hides to do its grieving. As far as I know, Léon doesn't talk about it, men don't talk about such things. Ambre distills her pain with her sister and Rose, and she looks after her nephews as if they were the fruit of her own womb. Aelis gladly let her have her sons, already as babies, when she had too much work to do, when the noise and crying exasperated her. She tried to console Ambre, too, in her way, clumsy and sincere, she admitted she wasn't happy, either, she didn't want them, her three sons, she wanted a daughter. It wasn't reasonable to hope for a girl in those times, even to help on the farm, girls were a worry until husbands were found for them, they were weak, when they worked the fields they weren't as fast or as strong as the men, they were too quick to cry, their health was unpredictable. But it would have been so sweet, a little girl in this house, murmured Aelis, closing her eyes not to see her boys anymore. But fate hadn't listened, because of the five children born to her, there were only males—arms to bend, backs to carry, brows to sweat. Aelis spread her hands in a gesture of resignation, then let them fall by her side.

Ambre lowered her gaze. It wasn't an issue for her, it was clear that she couldn't have children. It resonated in her hollow flesh. It hurt. She smiled. It doesn't matter, she said to herself, again, in silence. But it wasn't true, it did matter and it did hurt.

After her, and after Léon, there would be nothing. That was how lineages died out, how worlds were erased. Which way does misfortune lie, she thought, looking at her sister, and she said nothing, she hurried to take the youngest, still an infant, in her arms, she would learn to be content with this, she would have to.

The years have gone by and they're still at the same point, the two sisters, Aelis with her three sons and Ambre alone with her drunk. They manage as best they can, each on her own. They've preserved their complicity beyond the vagaries of life, and with their farms so close they're able to spend moments whispering together every day. We're lucky, said Ambre, but Aelis wanted more, she would have liked for all four of them, all seven of them now, to live in the same house, it would be better, it would be easier, to do the mending together, the cooking together, the cleaning together. Sleep in big beds side by side. Ambre laughs, says she's exaggerating, and Aelis insists, it's not unusual for families to share the same farm, young and old together, and since they no longer have their parents, and Eugène and Léon don't either, there's room, they could, she says, Ambre smiles, shrugging her shoulders. They live so near to each other, there's barely a hundred steps between the two houses, just the yard to cross. Aelis thinks that's still too far, and they both burst out laughing. They love these moments stolen from work, they sit side by side on the bench when the weather is fine, or in the dark room if the rain has chased them indoors. They have these joyful words, and always, with Aelis, these outbursts, she gets carried away, And what if Eugène died? And what if Léon died? Quickly, in a nice accident of the kind we see so often around here, and then they'll obey the custom that says a widow goes to live at her brother-in-law's, she doesn't mind, does Aelis, whether it's Eugène or Léon, and Ambre laughs again, it would be better if Eugène survived, all Léon knows how to do is drink, there's no trusting him. Yes, with laughter like this they can let themselves say anything. Beneath the laughter they murmur their distress, the fact they no longer live under the same roof, their disappointment with adult life.

What remains is essential, however: Ambre and Aelis have never lost their love for each other. Some afternoons when I'm drifting around the farmhouse I can hear the sisters' conversation from afar, and I can testify to it: just then, they're no longer two distinct personalities, but two identical rays of sunlight, and I understand that they are twins, truly, two women who are alike down to their smiles and their transfigured voices, overflowing with affection and merriment. The rest disappears in the space of a breath, a few words, their constantly renewed togetherness. With Aelis, her dissatisfaction with everything. With Ambre, her vile husband and the empty cradle, the money half drunk before it even reaches the house, the shouting matches Eugène overhears on evenings when he's rubbing down the big horse, and which he won't mention.

At our place, Rose, too, orders me around—Bran.

Tells me to sit back down.

Tells me to stop straining my ears to where the voices are coming from, it's none of our business, she murmurs, and I can see the sorrow in her eyes.

Rose has hung the shirts and rags out to dry, now she grabs me by the scruff of the neck and we come back inside the house in a hurry. Door locked, bolt slid closed. We listen. It's a sound we know by heart and yet every time, it makes us tremble. It's a sound that leaves us vulnerable. It doesn't happen very often, but it does happen. It's the one sound we hate: a horse galloping, the horse that belongs to Ambroisie's son.

In the village they talk about the master's son, and they say Ambroisie-Son. The Son is roughly Eugène's age. The Son has a gray horse you can hear coming from far away, with his very particular jerky gait—is it the breed, is it the heavy hand of his rider that upsets the horse; the countryside and the village are filled with this mixture of galloping and trotting and—

All of us, if we can, steal into the shadows and hide.

The Son is out of his mind.

We despise the masters, yet Ambroisie-Father is fair. He demands his due, he's a hard man, in his way, but he doesn't bleed us, doesn't keep a watchful eye on our crops or our women, doesn't come into our yards, or rarely, only when it's harvest time, or to request our labor for an unexpected task. The Father is not insane like the son, nor is the Mother, for that matter, no one knows where that madness came from. He rides about without guards, alone and frenzied, sure of his power, we make ourselves scarce in his presence, we make ourselves invisible.

One day the Son will be the master. We pray that the Father

will live to be a hundred, so that the Son will not come onto our lands to trample on our crops and ogle our daughters.

On the Ambroisie estate the men grow primarily wheat, rye, barley, and oats, depending on the season, and buckwheat too, which is hardier. At the beginning of summer they keep an eye out for anything that might endanger the coming harvest, and one of those dangers is Ambroisie-Son.

As if storms, drought, and frost were not enough, then, they'll cry, after the fact. The Son likes to hunt, all the masters like to hunt. But the Father never shows such scorn for our labor and our survival. He has never led his horses and his people hell for leather over our fields, hacking into the wheat, upending the oats, trampling on the buckwheat. But the Son—even the knowledge that the income from this wheat and these oats will be his, in part, does not stop him. He wants only amusement. If a hare or a roe lures him into our crops, he will follow. To hear his lunatic cries, the shrieking as he scolds his dogs, mingled with an uncontrollable, disturbing glee, we wonder whether his pleasure is not in fact intensified when the hunt includes the destruction of our lands. The Son spits on us. He is untouchable. He is the master.

We watch him riding his fine gray horse and we bite our lips. No one has dared try to reason with him, ever since one of the elders, Old Lazare, intervened one day and the Son ran him through with his sword. It took Lazare days to die. We can say nothing. Or we say it among ourselves. And then we fall silent. Perhaps it does us good to cry out, too, for something to come out, whatever is possible, because we'll never take up arms, only our words full of hatred, until shame silences us. We return one by one to our cottages while the women look on. That look, harder than the words that have just been said, that look falls on the men, men who bow their heads, who grimace because of the wheat, but the women—

The Son loves to hunt, and he loves our women. If they

don't hide quickly enough, the Son, galloping after his prey, suddenly swings his horse around, forgetting the fox or the stag he was after, and spurs his horse to catch up with a skirt, it matters little whether she's very young or far too old, a skirt is for lifting, the horse has not even stopped and already the Son has dismounted and is on her. It's his vice—more than a vice, an obsession, he loves women, he'll chase them for a spell to get them away from the farms, and then he'll hurl them into the grass. If they cry out he'll damage them, he likes that, too. We all know it. When the men in the woods or in the fields see the horse go by at a full gallop, they know. The women who hear the pounding of hooves and run to corral the children into the house, they know. No one talks about it. Afterwards, the women who have been raped smooth their homespun dresses and rub a cloth over their soiled bodies. They pick up their work where they left off, they let the children out, not saying a word, their gaze slightly lowered, their expression slightly darker. The men come home that evening and don't mention that they saw the horse that day, as if not speaking about it will make it impossible, as if looking away protects them and the earth can go on turning, things will vanish of their own accord in muted pain. When a child is born that resembles the Son, the family keep their mouths shut and kill the infant the following night.

Sometimes a woman fights back and Ambroisie-Son strikes her or teases her with the tip of his dagger. At times like this, there are traces, no one can ignore the fact that something happened. But it's the girl's fault. She didn't want to let him get away with it. She put herself in danger of her own accord, instead of waiting for the Son to have done with her, men's anger is now turned against her; when the tormenter is the master, it's easier to accuse the victim. In the evening by the hearth, a quick glance conveys reproach, and distance is kept. Time goes by, like an excuse. And the earth resumes its turning, slightly grayer, slightly lower, there's nothing to say so nothing is said.

I can hear Rose murmuring behind the shutters, her whispering mixed with the low growls of curses, as if Ambroisie-Son might hear us through the walls of the house. She looks out toward the top of the path, to see whether the gray horse is galloping up The Rises. I can tell she's praying that the young women, too, are safe inside, hidden, huddled together. Ambre, she is thinking, and Aelis.

Since I spend my days roaming around the countryside, I've seen the sisters, I know their hiding places and their tricks for when they hear the horse coming, and I'm not worried. They have a cry to warn one another, a shrill bird call, anyone would think it was a panicked blackbird. They've set up little hideaways in the area around the farms, or a bit further away for when, in autumn, they go looking for chestnuts or kindling wood: huts half buried beneath low-hanging boughs, false piles of tangled branches into which they can slip, deepened holes where they can wedge themselves until the horse and its rider are out of sight. There's a certain insolence to the twins, but there's no foolhardiness. They know they are beautiful. They're aware of the danger. No one here trifles with the masters, and women like them least of all, with their unusually slender figures—as a rule, only château-dwelling maidens have such finesse; peasant girls are stocky and solid, made for work.

But it's different with Aelis and Ambre. The long fair hair they only wish they could leave loose, its sunlit strands escaping from their kerchiefs; their eyes, too blue, and the sparkle of their laughter bubbling like the fresh spring up on the plateau, and yet again there are no words for it, it's in the gazes upon them, in the murmurs. This is their tragedy: if the Son comes to notice them, he will swoop down on them. From very early on, their father, then Eugène, and for a long time Léon, too, have been incessantly warning them. You must be on your guard, imagine that you are a doe alone in the woods and with every step you take you might meet a hunter. And that is something they have remembered.

And so Ambroisie-Son has never seen either of the sisters with his own eyes. Sometimes he has sensed their shadows in the distance, and perhaps he spurred his horse to go after them; but despite his steed's vivacity, the women had always vanished by the time he got there. The Son continued his chase, did not know what he had just missed, otherwise desire would have maddened him to the point of sniffing the tiniest burrows to flush the beauties out, just as if he were hunting game, walking next to his horse to stalk his prey, inscribing vast methodical concentric circles betraying a tenacity on the verge of rage. Except that Ambroisie-Son does not know Aelis, does not know Ambre. They laughed about it one day after a close call, when the young master tore through the countryside, a few steps from where they were holed up, and very nearly found them. That day I had left my hiding place. I remember the Son's eyes on me, but I didn't care, I had come out to draw that gaze of his, to distract it from the twins, who were too close by, who were breathing too loudly. Perhaps the Son hesitated, disappointed, enraged, he'd thought something else was in the offing; he put one hand on his crossbow and my heart began to pound. A few seconds went by. Then he yanked violently at his horse's mouth and rode away.

The Son must not lay a finger on Ambre or Aelis. Rose would not forgive me, even if it's not up to me to protect them. One day she told me that you have to be prepared to die for the people you love, she was thinking of her sons, but her sons have left the Hinterland and it's no concern of ours now. The world's an ugly place and there's nothing we can do. And yet in the middle of that despair there are sparks that no amount of woe can completely destroy—the laughter of children, the turnips you unearth to find they're not completely spoiled after all, the warm room at Rose's when I come in and ease my shivering from the chill outdoors.

There is the look between Ambre and Eugène on work days, still, that gaze I continue to steal and which heals everything. The moment I like best of all is in the evening, when there's no need for haste and Eugène sits on the low wall and takes the tumbler of water from Ambre's hands. He needn't stop to drink here: a hundred paces further and he'll be home, but this, too, is home, on this wall, with her and with me—and the big horse giving a shake, then nosing for grass, and we all fall silent. Those moments soften the brutishness of life. They spread a balm, and while it may not heal any wounds, it simply keeps everything from imploding.

We all know that life's not as it should be.

We are acutely aware of the world's imperfections; land could be shared equitably, and wealth and work and sickness. Love, too. But the world isn't a just place and never has been. We've always been paupers and we've always had masters. We don't know where it comes from. It's always been like this, no doubt. We don't know if we can change anything in that respect, not that we don't have the strength, but we just don't think about it. The master is the master.

Every layer of the world reigns like this over the layer just below. And even among themselves men are ruthless. The more prosperous peasants treat their workers like dogs, the craftsmen make slaves of their apprentices, parents order their children about from cradle to grave. No one protests, the strongest, the oldest, are always right. Life goes on, leading from one day to the next, and no one ever wonders whether it's fair; no one ever asks if there was a better way, and yet of course, there was a better way. But, well. It would have called for thought. It would have meant envisaging possibilities, and we don't know how to go about it, or if we're even interested. Sometimes it's better to preserve an unfair world where everyone knows their place rather than smash it all to pieces and no longer be sure of anything. What we have today, we have, even if it's not much to speak of. Folks always have something to lose, even if it's just their life. If you really think about it, the simple fact of a roof over your head is good fortune.

Food.

Warmth.

Too little of everything, too shoddy, but it exists. So is it really in our interest for the world to change? I can't explain it any other way, it must be this uncertainty that has led to mankind's ability to willingly suppress any urge to rebel. Five or six years ago, Ambroisie-Son raped Siméon's wife. As is often the case, no one knew about it; and no one would ever have found out if she'd been able to endure it. But she was fragile, weak in the head. A few days later she threw herself down the well—that's where they immediately went to look when Siméon raised the alarm in the village, saying he couldn't find her: when something goes badly wrong, the men hang themselves from our trees, the women throw themselves down our wells. Siméon was huge, fleshy, bad-tempered. We knew he beat his wife. There again, that's the way of the world, we take revenge for our own helplessness on those who are weaker than us. But in this particular case Siméon, who had lost his punching bag, had no intention of letting the matter rest. He wanted to complain to Ambroisie-Father, and when the villagers dissuaded him, he decided to go after the Son. No one will ever know if he was serious, if he would really have done something, we weren't going to take the risk. The peasants of La Foye locked Siméon in a pigsty. He was as nasty as a canker and they beat him until, black and blue and dying of thirst and hunger, he swore he wouldn't try anything. No one believed him. He was strangled. We protected masters who had no need of protection, in order not to risk something worse than the life we already knew. We opted for silence. We're cowards, but we're alive.

There it is, it's come. It's here, at our place. Rose looks at me as she says it, It's here. She knows, because this time there are eggs missing from the little barn. She knows because she looked askance at me, but I'm not the one who took the eggs, I don't steal, or not very often, and I'm lousy at it. I would have broken the eggs, trying to eat them, I would have had yolk on my nose, and bits of egg shell stuck somewhere. Rose has brought out the old pitchfork with its tines, we don't use it much anymore, again she says the dogs' barking isn't mean, she's still thinking it must be an animal, and not a very big one, because it's quick and wary and we've never managed to see it. She says a fox would have moved on by now, it's been that long, and besides, the hens don't seem bothered. So maybe it's a cat. Rose used to have a cat, I know she loved that cat and I don't want her to love a cat more than she loves me. I don't want to share the corner of the room with some creature that serves no purpose. Cats chase mice, says Rose, but we can eat mice if we have to, we already did one winter when all the granaries and cupboards were bare. Rose cut off their heads and legs and we put them on the embers to grill, it smelled good, just like any meat would smell, you just have to not think about the fact that they're mice.

But Rose isn't sure it's a cat. We would've seen it by now, those creatures are not that wild, they don't behave like this, as if they were more afraid of us than anything. Rose is saying it's a cat so as not to be afraid. Now it's stealing eggs. Now Rose is on edge. It has to stop.

When the dogs are barking up there at Eugène's or Léon's place, Rose says, adamantly, It'll be down here next. She sets out saucers with moistened bread to attract the animal, and she doesn't laugh anymore. That thing prowling around is a thief more than anything, and it's a matter of catching it. I don't like this upset in our lives, I don't like what's going on. I can sense something different that could forever affect the way we live. Deep down I'm like those men who shout that everything has to change and who, once they're on the verge of doing it, realize it wasn't so bad, before.

In the meantime, Rose has mentioned it to Ambre and Aelis, and they too have been listening to the dogs barking for days. There's a tension in the air. They believe in some harmless little creature, women come up with nice stories, they need to dream. The stories are like fever, or smallpox—contagious, you talk about it, and then everyone gets it, it clings to you and after that the problems begin, because of everything you didn't think about, everything that seemed so simple and that really isn't. Eugène doesn't believe in the wives' tales either. He shrugs and says that if this continues, they'll have to kill the cat, or whatever it is, because he cannot stand these nights cut in bits by the dogs' barking, which wakes his sons and leaves him exhausted already at dawn. Rose, Ambre, Aelis: they nod, puzzled. No one can recall there ever being such a presence—furtive, invisible, tenacious. It's new. It's both exciting and worrying. Eugène was born into a tough life: either something is useful, and you find a use for it, or it's useless, even harmful, and you get rid of it. The women eventually come round to his way of seeing.

Eggs are disappearing at our place every night, and now Rose is beside herself. She keeps placing saucers with moistened bread outside to trap the creature, it's not a game anymore, there's anger to it, the anger at being robbed, the anger, above all, at failing to understand. During the day we forget, there's too much to do in the garden or in the woods, but in the evening when she goes to count the eggs, Rose lets out a cry. When her legs aren't hurting too much, she leans against the wall inside the barn and waits until nightfall, but her presence is heavy and noisy. She stays until I come and look at her and she says, Yes, I know.

So Rose knows. That this is all so stupid, and it's taking up too much space in her head, she won't catch the creature.

But still. She goes back there at dawn and we pass each other just as I'm on my way up to wait for Eugène and his horse. When I come home, she tells me triumphantly that the saucer was empty, and I don't see what's so special about that, given that the creature is coming for our eggs anyway; and besides, it gets away every time, it doesn't care, all it leaves is the mark of its body in the old packed hay. Rose is exasperated, there's a sort of ridiculous pig-headedness about her, because she doesn't know how to hunt, doesn't know how to lie in wait. She searches corners, the obvious hiding places, knowing very well that the animal will rush out past her if she gets anywhere near its refuge. But nothing moves and she goes away with her empty saucer, disappointed. She thinks it's idiotic to waste this little portion of black bread, but that's why the creature has moved in to our place, that's why we even have a chance of catching it. And so she starts all over again.

One night she awakes before the dogs start barking. It's like an intuition. She listens out for the mutts to start whimpering on their tethers, the sound of their paws pacing back and forth over the ground, something inside her senses that perhaps, this time, something is coming. And so, with mindless impulsiveness she gets up, throws a shawl over her shoulders and hurries out. I follow her despite her warnings—if I make the slightest gesture, the least little sound—but I won't. She walks silently and the dogs, surprised, remain silent and watch as she crosses the yard. By the side of the barn, we stop short. There's the thought of danger, of vagrants, bad folk, all sorts who could be prowling around in these wretched times. Rose is holding the pitchfork, even though it is hardly reassuring.

We stand like two soldiers, motionless and invisible, and we wait. When you're waiting, time always seems to expand, and I don't know where I am anymore. I sit down. I'm doing as she told me, I'm not moving. I just keep my eyes wide open to try and see better, and I have no idea how much time has passed.

And then there's a sound. A rustling. A presence flowing past, perhaps. Breathing, a frenetic chewing, regularly interrupted by what I suppose are startled gestures, but I can't make them out, I'm huddled by the wall and I just know there's a presence. Instinctively, Rose has drawn her arm back to gain momentum with the pitchfork. She leans forward with infinite slowness, as much from fear the animal will get away as from fear alone, because it's rising inside her, what if it's more than an animal. At the same time I crouch lower down. We are not alone. There's the two of us. She moves forward, incredibly slowly, the pitchfork raised. And at that moment she begins to tremble, while her gaze shifts forward to sweep over the spot where she left the saucer, and she stops moving, drops the pitchfork in surprise. That instant when, in a flash, Rose identifies the tiny figure, first bent over the saucer then springing away with a hoarse sound that is nothing like a cat's meow. And Rose grabs me, holds me, pointlessly, I'm not moving.

Stunned, both of us.

It's much bigger than a cat.

Much wilder but also much more familiar, and I freeze, there it is, that thing, and just then I understand what was expanding around us, I understand why I felt that my life could suddenly change, why it has already changed, been swept away, split open in the space of two or three seconds—and that I was mistaken. It is not an evil thing that has come, it's just insane.

Crouching opposite us, unmoving in the dim light as if she were trying to make herself invisible, her lips drawn back over her baby teeth, is a little girl.

Two

It's been two years, nearly three, since Madelaine came into our lives. I still remember the night Rose and I caught her—because there's no other word to describe what we did to that wild little animal, no words could have reasoned with her. She was so agile and panicked, Rose tossed an old blanket over her head, and once she was trapped underneath, we fell on her. We captured her. We waited for her to tire, to gasp for breath, to fall motionless. Then we were able to take her—to drag her, more like—to the house, Rose locked the door behind us, and we looked at her.

We had no idea where she had come from. She didn't speak. She merely observed us, fiercely, and from her throat came sounds that belonged to an animal. I know that Rose wondered, for a moment, if this was a good idea, if what we had before us was really human. It looked like the devil. It spat and hissed like an angry snake, and yet it was an adorable little girl, we were both aware of that, she had a pretty face dotted with freckles and dirt, yes.

We kept her locked up for seven days. The house had never had the door closed for so long. The child was used to houses, that much we understood. She also knew how to speak, badly, but words did come. Rose said she was surely a hunger child, that's what we called them, the children who ended up on the roads or in the forests after their parents had died in a famine, no one wanted to take care of them, it was too hard to feed another mouth, hard enough to feed oneself. And that was how

Rose got the better of the girl, with food, that's how in three days, no more, Rose won her over, the girl was eating out of her hand. As for me I had nothing to give her. And yet the strongest, most immediate bond, the one that would last forever, even after Rose had given the girl to Ambre, was between the two of us. I knew right from first glance and I could see she knew, too: we were two of a kind. We were wild. We were different. Of course we could be tamed and educated, but that part of the unknown remained, that element inside us ready to burst at any moment, in her eyes and in mine there was a little flame that burned not quite straight, not quite clear, that no one would control.

And I wailed for a long time, when Rose took the child to Ambre's, two weeks after her arrival, I moaned as if they were tearing a part of my heart from me, we were already bound to one another. We couldn't keep the little girl, said Rose. Rose was too old. A mother was needed, not a granny, not a friend, and yet those first weeks when she was up there, she ran away to come and see me. We picked up our games where we'd left off the day before, we rolled together in the grass. I had gradually grown apart from Eugène's sons, they'd been put to work, and we saw each other only occasionally in the evening when it was not yet dark and they weren't too tired; but the little girl . . .

The little girl was always there.

She put an arm around my neck and we frolicked, running as fast as our lungs would carry us, and I beat her every time, but she didn't mind, she burst out laughing. She often took a tumble—she was reckless, wouldn't stop if the path fell too steeply as we raced madly along, or she banged her foot against a stone, or the ground was slippery after snow. She fell and got back up. I waited for her. We set off again in unison, we went too far, Rose scolded me. I could hear her calling but there was still a little ice-rimmed sunshine, a little wintry daylight, and we were making the most of the world, so I didn't answer.

Ambre named her Madelaine.

Ambre became a mother all of a sudden; Rose did not yield to my sorrow.

Ambre paid no attention to the looks they gave her the first time she took the little girl with her to the village, and she said, This is my daughter. Everyone knew Ambre had no children, and that this one wasn't hers. Just a stranger; there was no one missing in the Hinterland, and before long there was no end of whispering about the little girl's origins, no end of conjectures about her face, for it did, in fact, resemble Ambre's, the same fine features, the same beauty already sketched there. For sure, the word witchcraft was uttered somewhere, and just as quickly stifled, a word that brings bad luck, the women who'd said it now held their tongues, and after a few weeks or months had gone by, they'd grown accustomed to the little girl at her mother's heels—since they had all accepted that Ambre was her mother, it made things easier. In a word, one day Madelaine was there, was all.

I think Eugène suffered from it. It's not something you ought to say, to suffer from the presence of a child, and yet in his wide eyes I saw so much distress, so much forced happiness, for Ambre's sake, and for the first time, he was excluded from it all. It must be said that the day Rose and I went up there with the little girl as a gift, Ambre was on her own. Léon was making his clogs in the village, or drinking them, either way, after Rose had left, Ambre was there with the child and had no one to share with, no one to witness her joy full on, and this joy, she had to get it out, she had to shout it, sing it. Eugène was the first to come. He'd finished his day with Jéricho earlier than usual, and was walking wearily up the path. He was pleased, he had some time, a bit more than usual, time to stop and spend with Ambre. And Ambre was there, and with her was a brand new little person.

I was there, too. Rose told me to stay over there so the child wouldn't get away, so she wouldn't come running after us, so that the minute we let her go, up there, we wouldn't find her back at our place. So many things had been turned upside down those days. I hadn't been waiting for Eugène in the morning, the little girl took all my attention, filled all my time. When Rose opened the door to the house again for the first time, she ordered me to look after the girl. We could go out but I had to stay with her. I had to protect her. I had to bring her home. So there was no time to go with Eugène, and I forgot about him and the big horse, I was so filled with the little girl's company. Eugène had noticed. The first morning I ran into him again, he rubbed my head and looked surprised. I liked his smile, a little mocking a little kind, and he said, Well, look who's here.

So yes, I was there, and I was there, too, when Ambre was holding the child's hand and waiting for Eugène, that day when I caught the look in the man's eyes, the same as when Ambre's arms would go around Jéricho's neck: it was like sudden pain in his heart, but more than that, he felt dizzy and he had to reach out to catch himself on the low stone wall. Ambre let go of the little girl to support him and settle him, and deep down that was what Eugène had wanted, for her to be his, for her to be for him, he'd already realized that everything was about to change. That day, he placed his palms over his face to hide the confusion dancing in his blood, to gain some time, calm his staggering thoughts. Ambre's warm fingers stroked his, trying to see through them, What's wrong, said the low, gentle voice, what's the matter.

Eugène wasn't prepared. He'd never imagined that life could be any different than it had been these ten years, for her and for him, and the others around them, suddenly everything was off balance. But Eugène grew up here, he knows his lot, knows that he must accept his fate. That it's pointless to struggle, you have to yield to destiny, and quickly, otherwise you'll lose everything; the struggle is often worse than the yielding. So he smiled at Ambre and Ambre came into his arms, it was an impulse, they were carried away, Ambre toward joy and Eugène toward fear. They held each other close like a farewell, Eugène receiving everything all at once, joy doubt hope. He managed to take Ambre by the shoulders before leaving, managed to say that it was a good thing, that the little cat who was not a cat would be tamed, and then they'd see.

I don't know what they'll see. I know that Léon had no say in the matter, either, when he came back up from the village with his breath heavy and found the child in Ambre's arms, and it was all too late, Ambre had shown the little girl to Eugène, and then to Aelis. Just then he wasn't even sure he understood what was going on, he was trembling a little, unsteady on the bench where Ambre had sat him down to explain. He looked at her, then at the child, as if he was wondering if she were not a double, and why she hardly resembled Ambre, but still, and in the end he said all right, and we'll never know what he agreed to, then Madelaine went into the house and there she stayed.

That same day, earlier, Aelis had been there. Aelis with her eyes wide open, hurrying across the yard because Eugène had told her. Aelis knocking at the door, and her voice trembling her words whispered—a little girl, a little girl. That had been her dream. Ambre brought her in gently, they had to be careful, the child was wild and timid, but no need to say it, Aelis sat down by the entrance to the room, right on the floor, she saw the little girl and her face lit up. She laughed very quietly, a clear laugh, Ambre thought about their games by the river when they were children, a clear laugh like that. She sat down next to her sister. They looked at Madelaine who was not yet called Madelaine.

I would have given my sons to have a little girl, said Aelis, reaching for Ambre's hand.

And here she is.

As she grew, Madelaine kept the freckles on her nose, and some days by the river, where we're not allowed to go, I watch her rubbing them with water to try to remove them. She knows they won't go away. She does it anyway. It's because of Léon who makes fun of her. Léon tells her she has scat on her face.

Madelaine doesn't like Léon. Because of the wine. It came about very quickly. At first we thought Léon had mended his ways, he had wings for the little girl, he felt responsible, he got up early, then started turning clogs till evening. But it didn't last long, maybe two or three weeks, time enough to add a little to the purse that Ambre hid among the linens, time enough for Madelaine's presence to become banal. We don't know what happened, a mishap, an argument, or just craving: one day Léon went to work and came home drunk. Ambre thought, That's it then, here we go again.

When she sees him in the distance, coming up the path from the village, Madelaine holds her head high and sniffs loudly. I like these ways of hers, still animal, her stubborn, spiteful side, or other times when her playfulness has no bounds. She hasn't forgiven Léon for the slap he nearly gave her one day when she went up to smell the wine on his breath, a strange, acid whiff that made her wrinkle her nose, and Ambre abruptly yanked her away, just missing the clout that Léon, enraged, had aimed her way. That was in the early days of Madelaine living with them, she had no manners no restraint, and it took Ambre several days to calm her down and keep her at the table when Léon was there.

Nowadays Madelaine can control herself, but she has these wild instincts inside, fierce gestures that are taking time to fade. Ambre is often afraid for her, because she's still small and rather delicate. I don't see why she should be afraid for her, when we mess around and sometimes we get really annoyed with each other, we fight like mad, we bite and scratch and it leaves long red streaks on Madelaine's skin, and bloody marks on my ears. One day Madelaine poked one of Léon's dogs in the eye because it had nipped her on the arm. There's no way to contain her: it's an eye for an eye, it's the law of the strongest. It's probably this urge that helped her survive, and it has stayed rooted in her guts. But little girls don't behave like that, and Ambre has been trying for a long time to make her listen to reason. By wearing her down, or even punishing her to make her understand. Put her outside. Out you go. She slams the door on the girl, who finds herself all alone without shelter, like before.

Madelaine screams. She cries, she scratches at the wood, begging to be let in. She presses against the latch. I don't know how Ambre can bear it, behind the door, how she resists, if it were me I'd open that door, I can't stand hearing the little girl sobbing, it tugs at my heart. I can picture Ambre with tears in her eyes, she knows she mustn't give in, that sweetness has no purchase on fury. I can just see her, leaning her brow against the door, her face haggard, eyes closed, fists clenched.

Then Madelaine goes off. Only the countryside will eventually wear her out, stifle her rage, and she runs through the forest, she strikes the trees with branches, breaking them one after the other, she scrabbles at the soil with her bare hands. At some point I go and join her. No need to speak, no need to say a thing, just the looks we give each other, that's enough. Come, she says, and I know it will be all right. In the beginning she would turn her back on me. I followed her because I was still thinking of what Rose had told me, that I had to protect her, and she would turn and insult me, but I went with her all the same. She ignored me and yet, from time to time, I could see that she was watching me out of the corner of her eye, to make sure I was still there. I was still there. That's what friends are for. Friends don't desert you. We eventually sat down side by side, and she pressed against me. I didn't move, so that those moments would last as long as possible.

Madelaine's escapades are the blue hours. Blue is the color of happiness, says Rose. It's a promising sky, it's water refreshing us, it's a gleam of light on a cloud that makes us feel peculiarly good. So I'll go for blue. The color of wildflowers. Of Madelaine's irises when she looks at me and starts to laugh, and her laugh is like the stream where there's a little waterfall, before you get to the Basilic, when we're already far from home. I'd like to tell Rose, those days when we get home late, that we left because of the blue, it was the blue calling us, maybe the horizon, too, has a color. We walk side by side and we listen to the world. Only the sound of our steps on the leaves in the undergrowth connects us to reality—otherwise we would fly, like runaway birds, we would go high in the sky and we too would have wings of blue. No one knows how far we go. We're not here anymore.

And then evening comes, we go home and life takes hold of us again.

Ambre shouts, because she thought Madelaine was lost. Rose shouts, because I didn't bring her back, but actually I did, I did bring her back, just not on time, is all, not early enough for her worrying. That's just the way we are.

Since Madelaine often sneaks out, before long Ambre gives her a knife. It's dangerous to give such a thing to a girl like Madelaine, but Ambre says it's less of a risk than letting her go defenseless along the paths and through the forest. Ever since we brought back two skinned fish from the river, Ambre has realized that we've been roaming much further than she'd thought. Madelaine loses the knife only a few days later.

So Ambre asks Eugène, Eugène who was shoeing the big horse at the forge, she asks for a piece of metal and he makes a little hatchet, a war weapon—for a little girl, a touch too heavy, but Madelaine will grow. On seeing the hatchet her face lights up. We'll never know why the implement seems so immediately familiar to her, why she wears it at her waist and never takes it off. She learns to use it, uses it for everything, even things that don't need an axe. She is terrifyingly skillful, the weapon is like an extension of herself. Eugène shows her how to sharpen it, how to hone an edge sharper than the sharpest knife. She slices small pieces of wood slantwise so that I can see. Now she can throw the weapon into a tree from five yards away, or ten; she can carve arrows and lances with disconcerting ease; to impress her cousins she performs a twirling number with incredible moves where she seems to dance with her hatchet, handling it with disturbing speed, where girl and weapon move as one, shining in the sun, rending the air with cries of joy. Sometimes we can hear Germain and Madelaine, how they're overcome with elation—Germain in his work, Madelaine as her weapon whirls and spins, and their laughter travels through the forest, through the countryside, across the fields bordering the village: the peasants raise their heads.

Madelaine and I continue to roam, our escapades taking us ever farther despite our thin bodies. The fire inside us. We want to be strong. Madelaine is the one who says it: we're afraid of nothing. When we hear the Ambroisies on the hunt, we hide, but not from fear. The smell of danger excites us. We roll in the humus so the dogs cannot scent us; we bury our breathing in the earth. We become leaves, mud, compost. We are fragrant with mushrooms and manure. We follow the hunters in the absurd hope they will leave us an animal we can eat; but they always take them all, slung over their horses' flanks, and sometimes as we lie in ambush behind thick shrubbery we watch them go by with all that food pounding to the rhythm of their gallop. I'd like to throw myself onto it; Madelaine stops me with her hand.

I want meat. A huge, insane, all-consuming craving. Madelaine says that if we had never tasted it, we wouldn't miss it. Yes, but. I recall pieces of pork, a hen that was stolen as well, not here, and even the smell of the grilled mice, and my head spins. If Madelaine would let me jump on the hunters' horses, not only would I take the hare and the deer, I would take the stallion, too. With their round rumps, stallions are better fed than we are, they eat our wheat, our bread, our bran. I think about all that flesh straining under their hide, about the portions it would make, our teeth closing over it, the haunches roasting on the spit. In recent years the harvests haven't been that good, we've had less to eat in our bowls, and meat is rare. So that is bound to sharpen my senses and make my head spin. The tightrope we are walking on is about to break, but as long as we can fill our bellies, just barely, I look elsewhere, and gradually the craving subsides; we won't eat Ambroisie's horses. In the village none of us dares to admit how gnarled and dry we are, while the masters have flesh on their bones. That too is just the way of things. You just mustn't think about it. Sometimes I wonder how the peasants can dig, hoe, turn over the earth, mow, and bring in the crops, when their food is so meager. What fire enables them to endure, what need takes them beyond their strength? The answer is in the dark circles under their eyes, in the hollowness of their gaze—exhaustion, fatigue, weariness. They are hardly worth more than the oxen they goad to keep them moving until they collapse, and they go home in the evening dragging their feet, dragging their arms, their gaze is empty, they sit at the table, they fall asleep at the same time as the children. The women stay up, together, and yet the days don't spare them: looking after the children who are too young to help in the fields, who are in their feet and clinging to their skirts; they're busy with work at home, the countless chores of washing, cleaning, mending and cooking, but also reigning over the farm, feeding the fowl and anything else in the yard or the barn—pigs, nanny-goats, sheep, if they have them. Not to mention the hours they spend in the vegetable garden, and working the land when the men summon them, when the season calls for it and extra hands are needed.

When I come home in the evening, I know how lucky I am. Rose never leaves her house and the room is always warm, with the soup always on the stove. We eat, and I'm happy with leftovers. I don't want to get used to eating well, or even better than what's usual. Sometimes, yes, if I can't take it anymore, a piece of hard lard or an egg stolen from the hens. But my belly mustn't think it's won the battle. It mustn't think that my ribs will stop showing because one day there was a slice of pork, you don't know what tomorrow will bring. Other people, to supplement their days, turn to poaching. They're right to do so. Rose doesn't poach. She wouldn't know how. She's too old. From time to time someone brings her a bird they've just killed, in exchange for one of her ointments or her healing—a blackbird, a thrush, a pigeon. But as a rule, we eat poorly, and little. You might say we eat just enough. Nothing more. Never more.

We spend our empty days wandering around the forest. In this winter season, there's not really anything better to do. When the weather permits, we collect dead wood, but most mornings the branches are stuck together by the bite of frost, we can only separate them by banging on them with other pieces of wood. Madelaine's hands are so chapped they bleed. Ambre wraps them in worn rags, rubs a bit of lard over them in the evening. It is so cold that the villagers have exchanged their rigid clogs for leather shoes with triple laces, supple ankle boots stuffed with handfuls of hay, but there's nothing for it, their feet freeze and the shoes get soaked, we put them by the fire to dry and the leather cracks all too soon.

For us, every winter, the cold weather also means meeting up again. Germain, Artaud, and Mayeul aren't working now, either for their father or on the Ambroisies' land, the fields are frozen. The masters have work for the adults, but the children are sent home: they don't want to feed them for nothing. For all that up to now they were useful at small tasks of cleaning, gathering, or picking, painstaking chores that nevertheless require less strength, now if it's just for charity they're not wanted, not even Germain with his colossal willpower. Everyone has returned home. And so in spite of the frost chilling us to the bone, we meet up every day to roam around the woods. Of course we don't go out for as long as in summer. Germain says we're like animals, our rhythm slows, our bodies sleep a little, in their way, numbed and fragile. And we have a quest: we have to bring home something to eat. A pretext for our games and our running, ever further, as if we had exhausted the resources of the land around The Rises and we have to go beyond to find herbs or berries that are still edible, or a little animal we might succeed in catching. The thought of going home later and finding a cheery fire and a piece of bread is enough to make us joyful.

We trek across the wooded hills, our breath barely warm, and we run to get warm, we pretend to fight, we remove the frost from our eyelids. Of course we have to find something to eat, but that doesn't stop us from playing, thinking about nothing, looking out at the world. Some afternoons when the sky is blue and we're dazzled by the snow reflecting the sun, we hear a bird cry and we know we're not alone.

Madelaine and Germain often walk ahead, scouting for anything that can be eaten or put to good use at home. They're the most determined, the most eager. Artaud, Mayeul, and I are the followers. We carry. We help. They send us to scout, pull, pick up, bring back, and on we go. It suits us. It's when we're on our way home, just when we can see the farms from the forest, that we have our race. We look at each other like horses held at the starting line, snorting and stamping our feet, waiting to see who will break away first. Our wild gaze sweeps from left to right, anticipating the signal, but no one dares, we wait for the best moment, the surprise, which will give us a stride or two or five in the lead. Often we jostle one another. Germain shoves Madelaine and Artaud in the shoulder, slows them down; they pull him back, circle around him, quiver. Mayeul and I stay well behind, we don't interest them. Mayeul because he's younger and never wins; me because, whatever happens, I'm the fastest. They shake their heads, they say it doesn't count. The winner is whoever gets there first after me. It doesn't matter. At some point we drop everything we've found, we'll come back and get our meager treasures afterwards, we are overwhelmed by the challenge: and we run. The first to touch the little wall at the edge of the path, on the other side of the yard between Eugène's and Léon's farms.

Our cavalcade has left us breathless, our voices shrill. Once we reach the wall Germain lets out his booming laugh, he always says he's the winner, even when it's Madelaine or Artaud, but most often it is him, he has a bigger build, yes, and he's taller, as well. When the other two manage to throw him off balance at the starting line, they're in with a chance. I listen to them while we retrace our steps to fetch our little bags, which are three quarters empty. Their voices are animated, the sound rises in the air, like a stream when it's not frozen, or the winter wheat when the winter allows it to grow.

Most often we pass by Ambre's farm first. Madelaine runs ahead, we hear a cry. Every time, Ambre puts her arms around her, holds her close, tight; in the beginning she would lift her up in her arms and whirl her around, just to hear the little girl laugh, but now Madelaine is a little bigger, and a little heavier, Ambre lets out a laugh, she can't do it anymore. And so she holds her tight. I always watch. I don't think any of us have ever been held like that. Maybe because Madelaine is a girl, and we're not girls. Aelis embraces her like that, too. Germain shrugs his shoulders, Those are women's ways, he says, a touch of jealousy in his voice. And yet, what would he do with them, those hugs, if his mother lavished them upon him, other than turn away and look embarrassed, the others would make fun of him, and if she cuddled them all, they'd try to get out of it, they're not children anymore, is what they're thinking.

And they're not girls, either.

Madelaine is tender and wild. She nestles up to you, puts her arms around you, kisses you. Then all of a sudden she runs off. She goes back to her world. She'll pick up a stick and threaten us if we snicker, when we sit on the wall off to one side in a group, never for long, we'll soon go back to our games with her.

Aelis and Ambre look at us. Look at her. It's hard to know, really. The only thing I'm sure of is that they didn't gaze at us that way when it was only Germain, Artaud, Mayeul, and me. So. We could feel bitter, but there's too much joy, too much spirit in that little girl for us to hold anything against her. There's only one word that no one says, yet that's the word that has bonded us all these years: we love each other, is all. Each one of us thinks that he loves, or is loved, more than the others. There's no answer to that. Our relations are interwoven like threads, from one to the other. If this love were a spider's web, we would be the flies trapped inside it, but we wouldn't die. It would be a web to hold us together, not to consume us.

Madelaine is a daughter to Ambre and Aelis. She's a daughter for both of them. They share her, they hand her back and forth from kisses to cuddles. There's a piece of Madelaine for Ambre, and one for Aelis. Through her, their close bond is reinforced, their hands spread wide for her. With us it's different: the greatest compliment we can give her is that Madelaine is our brother. Our brother in arms, our brother in the woods, in games, in races. We see no difference between her and us, and that's how she's growing up, shoved about, teased, punched and cuffed as much as we are, since she's part of our tussles and fights and brawls, but we're wary of her, she's the tetchiest of us all. Sometimes Germain wrestles a bit too rough with her. He acts as if it wasn't on purpose. I see her holding back her tears, holding back her fists. She's looking for a way to get back at him. If he were an enemy, she'd find a way to kill him, there on the spot, the flame is quivering in her gaze. But it's only Germain, and she has no solutions that don't hurt, she champs at the bit, and Eugène's sons have no idea how much violence she is restraining deep within at such moments. Maybe Artaud does, he's waiting for it to subside, he's studying the girl's features. Afterwards, when it's possible to go near her again, he puts an arm around her shoulder and in a low voice he tells her she's his favorite.

The forest is our playground, and yet we're not playing as much as we used to. Is it because we're slowly making our way into adulthood? Because we're growing more sensitive to the hardships of life eating away at our spirit, wearing down our strength? What energy we have left we put into our work and into what is useful. Our running and shoving have become a mission: still the same, find something better to eat, or some dead wood to add to the hearth. By the end of the season, when there's not enough fodder, Mayeul and Madelaine take the two pigs to the woodland pasture. Yet more and more often Eugène's sons, and even Madelaine, don't leave the farm at all, there's so much to do. Repairing, cleaning, feeding, going for water, turning the earth in the vegetable garden—all these little chores strung together keep us busy from dawn to dusk. The days go by, sluggish. We meet up at the end of the afternoon, before it gets dark. When fatigue hasn't got the better of us, we hurry into the woods. The forest revives our childhood. Madelaine pauses, spreads her arms, spins around. She feels the calm of the tall trees. Quite often we sit for a moment in silence, not so much from exhaustion as to melt into this familiar place: the forest is our garden, our country, our roots.

Madelaine leads the way. She has gone too far. Germain reminds her, we mustn't go beyond the clearing of old beech trees, but she doesn't care, she keeps going, she wants to see the château, and the woods are protecting her. It's because of the hunt that Eugène's sons hesitate. They can picture Ambroisie's men barreling out on their horses, not leaving us time to hide. If we're in their way, the horsemen won't stop. The same applies to people as to the tilled fields: they are less important than the masters' pleasure. Madelaine gives a shrug. The forest is not forbidden. Germain knows it's not a question of rights, simply one of danger, we can keep going but it will be at our own risk. He doesn't want to look like a coward, so he walks ahead of Madelaine. I can tell from the tension in his features that he is listening to the sounds of the world. We've all heard of accidents. Peasants, often women or children, knocked down by the horses, trampled, crushed.

And yet the forest excites us. In the places where our folk don't venture, it has more to offer. There's wood that hasn't been gathered, and mushrooms and berries. And when the weather is fine we sometimes find wild fruit—apples or plums—and we fill our satchels, eyes shining, and our hearts are pounding, even if none of us admits it. We move like thieves, quickly and fitfully, as if we were allotted only so much time in that place. We're on a raid, we'll rake up everything we can. And then—there's no other word for it—we flee. Once we're in a safer place, closer to the farms or the village, Germain begins to laugh. We jump up and down, we have triumphed—over what we don't quite know—we're thinking of the moment when we'll set our treasures down on the table. How happy the women will be—Rose, Aelis, Ambre. Were it not for Madelaine we'd never have gone there, but this we don't admit.

Today it's raining. The air is softer and the drizzle has been seeping onto our shoulders and backs since morning. The earth sticks to our feet and we have left the empty plots, we'll begin plowing later, spring is still a ways off. No one really wanted to run in the forest but the hours have been passing too slowly in our dark houses, we've been going around in circles. I was the first to go out and I joined Madelaine; we went up to the last farm where Eugène's boys were also feeling bored, so we set off, with our cloaks still damp, we won't be bringing any wood back, we're just going on the off chance. Once we're some distance away we start looking at the ground. All we can hope for at this time of year are chanterelles. After the first few warmer days you can spot them among the leaves, Germain knows where to look. That's why we have our noses to the ground.

That's also why we didn't see it, didn't expect it, we were focused, searching the earth, I mean: we didn't do it on purpose. It wasn't us who . . .

It just came there.

It startles us, we hear it without hearing, we're thinking about the sound of our footsteps on the leaves; and we hear other steps in with ours, and we're afraid, all of us without exception, when suddenly it appears before us, in a flash. It's still only a shape, just there, we didn't realize, but Madelaine instinctively reaches for her hatchet and hurls it with all her might to defend us. There's a sound, and then it falls. She has pierced the deer's throat.

Now all five of us surround the body lying on the white grass. One after the other we look at the deer and we look at each other. We look at Madelaine.

Madelaine.

Murmured Artaud, his eyes wide and worried.

Germain sways on his feet, undecided. More than undecided: terrified. This is something we do not have the right to do. It is forbidden to hunt on Ambroisie land. The hunt is reserved for the masters. Those who poach know what they risk if they are caught: they will be killed the way they killed the masters' game. Those who do poach take little animals that are easy to hide under their loose shirts. Birds, sometimes hares. But we . . .

That's why we must make it clear: we didn't do it on purpose.

The deer is lying there before us, it seems huge, and we cannot decide whether to leave it. Several silent minutes go by. Mayeul wipes his hand over his face. He says, What shall we do? Then Madelaine, staring at the dead animal, bends down to pick up her hatchet. On standing she says what we all want to hear and don't dare say, it goes too far back in our memory. She murmurs,

We're going to take it home and eat it.

The words are like a terrible flash in our heads, as if lightning had struck just next to us and was pulling us from our lethargy. Germain stands up straight. He says, That's impossible.

Why? Madelaine protests, and yet she knows why, of course she does. Germain explains all the same. He knows she knows but we need for him to say it, because of the temptation. So we just leave it here? Artaud silences Mayeul with his hand. Germain says, Let's go, come on, let's go. There is this rising fear—if the masters were to come through here on the hunt, since they have nothing else to do except go hunting. We're going home, Germain says again.

We're on the alert. We turn around, at the same time, with the same urgency. Except for her. Madelaine steps away from Germain's grip when he goes to grab her arm. We hear him whispering, You're out of your mind, completely. We've already realized from the look in Madelaine's eyes that she won't give in. But neither will Germain, he's very aware of the risk, of his younger brothers there with him. This is what is dividing us, we can feel it.

Help me, Madelaine says, and Germain shakes his head.

Help me, then go home, she says, so he lifts the carcass and slings it over her frail shoulders. He grabs his brothers' hands. Before leaving he tries one last time. You won't manage. They'll catch you.

Her face is lit with a fierce joy, a raging smile on her lips. She ignores Germain, she looks at me. Are you coming, Bran? And I stay with her, her little steps hindered by her burden, her back bent to the weight of the animal. I can see her jaws are clenched fit to break, her eyes red with effort, or with anger, but the tension is too great for the anger to emerge, she has to keep up her strength, she grits her teeth and keeps walking. In no time Germain, Artaud, and Mayeul have disappeared. They're walking quickly, fear giving them wings. The forest closes around them and we are here, Madelaine and I, consumed by silence and her labored breath, there's nothing I dare try to do but wait for her. I look around at the vanishing daylight. I think about what has just happened, moments filled with more emotion and danger than all the years of life before Madelaine. The girl disturbs me, too, sometimes, but she fascinates. We do things we had never imagined doing. We think about things that are unthinkable. I feel a knot growing, deep in my gut. The farther we go, the more the knot gives way to a sort of uncontrollable fire. Night is gently falling, and I feel almost happy, looking at Madelaine struggling to carry those fifty pounds of meat; we've been walking for over an hour. She's going more and more slowly, but she's still going.

And suddenly there's a rustling of footsteps in the forest and we freeze. A figure in the distance. Coming toward us. We stand as straight as possible, as if it will help us to see better. A few seconds go by and I feel it, how at last Madelaine is frightened. It's impossible to hide in the forest, bare with winter, and the man coming toward us has already seen us. He's almost running. Oh, says Madelaine, and I can hear the breath go out of her all at once, and I recognize him.

Eugène is here.

I don't move, and Madelaine senses that there's no danger, until she too can see him clearly, she almost cries out his name. Eugène walks toward us, he doesn't need to tell us that his sons had told him, we already realized. I feel Madelaine shrink closer to me, recoiling to avoid a slap, but it doesn't come. Eugène gazes at us and he seems so tall. We're in his shadow. A moment earlier, I thought we were invincible.

His deep voice in the forest.

He looks at Madelaine, he looks at the deer on her back.

He says: Give it here.

Madelaine doesn't object, lets Eugène take the deer from her. He props the animal on his powerful back, so different from the little girl's, where the animal overwhelmed her. Eugène does not flinch, does not falter. He takes Madelaine's arm, looks at me. He doesn't tell us we have to hurry, he doesn't need to, his quick steps oblige us to follow him at a trot. I can see how Madelaine is looking at him, the way I do, fascinated by this strength that surpasses us, even when we have no deer to carry. We are breathless as we run after him, sometimes he looks back, but doesn't slow down: he stretches out his hands to us, rather like a woman calling to the farm animals when she's tossing vegetable peels to them, and we make an effort, a small burst of speed as we run. Half an hour or more, the day is turning gray. We're at the edge of the forest and Eugène comes to a halt. At the end of the plateau opening before us is a small field gorged with rain, he points to his farm and turns to Madelaine. Go have a look, he orders. Come back and tell me if there's anyone.

Madelaine spurts ahead to scout around. The winter twilight has driven everyone indoors and she waves to us. Come on, says Eugène, and we join her, turning off toward the barn where the big horse is dozing.

Jéricho, murmurs Eugène, to warn him of our arrival.

The horse sniffs the scent of blood. His master kneels at the other side of the barn and begins at once to cut up the meat with a long knife. Madelaine keeps watch by the door. It all feels so deserted.

She asks.

About his sons.

Eugène says he sent them further away, sent them to dig a hole, despite the rain, in a place where the soil is thick and rich, a hole for the carcass, for afterwards. Eugène is skilled with a knife but he's not used to cutting up deer, that we can see. He hesitates along the bones, carves out thick strips, leaving flesh on the skeleton, then goes over it a second time. His hands are trembling slightly. If we get caught now, it will be impossible to say we are innocent. We've gone too far. My eyes are stinging, I'm that terrified by the smell of flesh.

Eugène rolls the pieces of meat up in some old cloths and hands some of them to Madelaine. That's for your mother. That's for Rose. Go, now, go home. Eat all you can. Don't keep anything. Then heat some acidic herbs for the smell. Tell Ambre to leave the paws of the rabbit I caught two days ago out on the stove, that will cost us less, if ever. Above all, not a word. Say nothing to Léon. When Léon's been drinking, he comes out with everything. Mix the meat with the turnips and tell him I poached a hare, he won't know the difference, drunk as he is.

We leave the barn, Madelaine and I, and we run into Germain pushing a wheelbarrow; then we hear the remains being tossed into it. We don't look back, any of us. We never saw one another. Fear has us in its grip, thrilling.

Later, Madelaine will ask her cousins where they buried the remains of the deer. She wants to go and see the spot at the edge of the woods where the earth has been pressed down, leaves and twigs scattered over it to make the hole invisible, she'll search and of course she'll find it, because they told her where to look, but otherwise she'll assert that you can't tell a thing. We'll smile together, our senses still exhilarated by the meat we've eaten, the way Eugène told us to, all in one go, the smell is too recognizable when the flesh has been grilled. We stuffed ourselves, all of us, even me, filled fit to burst, enough to give us a stomach ache, but it brought so much happiness to feel those cramps from overfilling our bellies, we felt our strength return, and never mind if it was an illusion, that sensation of fullness. We were all thinking that at the Ambroisies' château, they're fed like that every day.

Even the Son's gray horse eats meat, murmured Artaud, or so he'd heard in the village, and we made fun of him.

Three days went by before we spoke about it among ourselves. Three days during which we lived with the terror of discovery, and yet there was nothing left to expose us, the meat had all been eaten, the skeleton was buried. But it stayed between us. We had transgressed. We are gods and paupers—without the makings of heroes, without assuming the consequences, we had dared. During those three days, whenever we met one another, in silence, we relived that afternoon that saw us dancing on the rope between life and death.

Or so we believed.

Because, tell me, what happened?

Nothing, absolutely nothing.

And surely that's what's hardest to believe, and most terrifying, that nothing happened. Until the moment we gave the bones to the dogs, until the moment when the extremity of our bellies rejected the meat in steaming little piles, we had been telling ourselves that Ambroisie's soldiers were about to barge into our farms. That we'd been seen, that we'd been denounced, that chance, too—but, no. We ate the meat and we are alive. That is what has marked us more than anything, the astonishing discovery that we could break the rules without anything happening. Never before had Eugène, or his sons, or I killed a deer. We've poached hares and birds, like everyone, less than everyone, and we all know that if we were to get caught, we'd get out of it by paying compensation or receiving a good walloping, often both at the same time: in a way, the punishment makes the risk worth it. But a deer. That is something else. Knowledge passed down from father to son, from house to house, without even saying a word, it's practically innate: you do not touch the masters' animals.

But Madelaine doesn't know anything. She just acts, is all.

Madelaine says, I'm hungry, and she eats.

So of course, as a result, the way Eugène's sons and I see her has changed. Because even if we wept with joy, chewing that thick venison, we knew it was folly, and a mistake. It was only afterwards that we realized to what degree. Before, we were still in a state of shock, caught up in the momentum, life allowing us to get carried away. Maybe the wisest among us was Germain, who began by turning his head not to see the dead deer and not to imagine the flesh inside it; after that, everything went too fast, and Eugène, when his sons told him, Eugène thought only of saving Madelaine, who would not let go of her catch. Helping Madelaine meant helping her with the deer. If it had been entirely up to Eugène, he would probably have ordered his sons to dig a slightly bigger hole and put the entire animal in there, with its haunches and its roasts, he wouldn't have taken the time to carve it up, wouldn't have run the risk of cooking it. That's where everything got out of hand.

Eugène doesn't really know why it happened this way. The moment he found Madelaine and me in the forest, and she raised her clear eyes to him, at that point there was no more anger in her, just exhaustion, like an ant dragging a seed twice its size, that exhaustion and yet a joyfulness as well—that is what Eugène saw. He didn't have the heart to . . . He took the deer on his shoulders and he brought it back to The Rises. He felt sorry for Madelaine—well not exactly sorry, it went much deeper than that, he'd had his breath taken away by her audacity. He couldn't help but admire her, even knowing he mustn't, anything but, that she would bring our downfall. But that was it. He saw himself next to this girl, with submission printed in his blood, and he was ashamed. He saw Madelaine's fierce determination, or her courage, it was impossible to send his sons to bury the meat, it would have been like whipping a horse that has worked itself to its knees all day long to finish its task; like drowning a cat that has just escaped the turbulence of a river, and he couldn't.

That didn't prevent the regret, or the fear, or the feast.

Simply, you mustn't do it again, and he told her three days later, that's not for us. Do you understand?

Madelaine doesn't understand. She hears but already her anger is returning. Her belly remembers the meat her mother prepared, still rare so they would eat it quickly, her teeth remember the flesh they tore at, chewed, swallowed, her gums are itching. Not for us, that means nothing to her, she doesn't want to accept it. Sitting next to me on a piece of wood she gazes at the horizon. I know it well, that stubborn profile of hers, eyes in a frown, the gleam in her pupils. It's what I like about her, her integrity, the way she finds openings. If it can't be done in a gentle way, it will be done forcefully. To dare, she murmurs, and she turns to me. I say nothing, of course. I know it, it's the women who rebel. In all my memories of the time I've been here, it is only the women who have sometimes raised their voice, raised a pitchfork or a stick to defend the simple possibility of living. They are prepared to shed their blood for their children. As for the men, they submit. They get used to everything. They don't want to die.

I look at Madelaine out of the corner of my eye, maybe this is the way Eugène looked at her. She is proud, hot-headed, so small, too, but we are all on the small side, the elders tell us that we're not growing because we don't have enough to eat. There is so much love in the way I look at her. And this strange perception behind that gaze, murmuring yes, we love Madelaine, she's a fire where we can warm our hands, a sun making our meadows fragrant.

She's dangerous.

To herself, and to us.

If we had wings, she would burn them.

Winter has settled in and we haven't seen any more deer. The cold numbs life, seizes our lungs when we go out and the air rushes down our throat. Sometimes we stay cloistered in the house until noon, but the houses themselves aren't warm anymore, frost has enveloped every stone on every wall, Rose places her hand there, shivers, adds a log to the fire. Of course we have to keep an eye on our supply of wood, and we count. The days from now until spring, if spring comes. There are mornings we no longer believe in it. There are mornings we no longer go out.

With the chill, all kinds of little rodents come looking for a way to survive in our buildings. Field mice, wood mice, shrews, all the creatures that don't hibernate are trying to get in the house. They must have been sheltering in burrows that eventually froze, curled up in hiding places that no longer protect them from anything. And now they're here. In our homes, we all pursue them mercilessly. We cannot let them eat our last bags of flour and, as I said, Rose and I have found a good use for them, since they end up in our soup. But they rummage and ferret and dig, and always manage to steal something, particularly in the outbuildings, which are not guarded. We have resigned ourselves to bringing our reserves into the house, what's left of them. It leaves an odd impression to sleep up against bags of wheat or crates of turnips. Rose said that if I eat them during the night she'll have my hide. She has been reduced to treating the villagers for nothing, rather than let them die. Hunger is beginning to come after us. One or two infants, an old woman. And it's only January.

We're familiar with this cold weather, and the hunger that goes with it. We lack everything, abundance has fled. We're happy when a season allows us to eat until the following summer, that's what we're used to. The cycle of hunger follows the cycle of seasons, and that seems normal to us; but when the balance is upset, when the periods of fine weather become fewer and hard times take up more and more room during the year, the men are fearful. And yet they're not asking for much, they were born making do with little, they have submitted to this strange order of the world that allots profusion and opulence to the masters alone. All they can do is survive. When the winters begin badly, they fall silent. They wait. We all wait.

The elders have predicted that the polar wind will drop, they talk about the color of the sky, the direction of the air, a barely perceptible sensation, but the countryside has not thawed in nine days and we find it hard to believe them. But we must cling to that hope, otherwise we'll all end up falling asleep in our cold houses by the fireplace that can no longer heat the walls, and so we move closer to the fire, at the risk of being singed by an ember during the night. But one morning the sky is low and we tell one another that the elders were right; the air smells of snow, the cold is going to loosen its grip. Above all, old Magne, who said that the frost was too intense, old Magne is going to light his oven, and we'll have fresh bread again. Finally, the evening soup won't be thickened only with flour, there will also be loaves and slices and mouthfuls to mix with the broth; the entire village is buzzing with expectation, Rose has brought out the leaven.

Like all the children in La Foye, the days I like best of all are the bread days. Days when the oven is hot from early morning to sunset, and the scent of perfectly toasted crust wafts through the air, with the enticing smell of baked flour, and there's a certain feeling of exuberance. It fills me with bliss. Over the long months I've been waiting for these days, when the old man agrees to light the oven, and he keeps an eye on it, checks the loaves, makes sure they're baked through. Everyone comes together. The oven takes too much wood for only one family to use it at a time, the inertia of the stones uses up the heat, so we've agreed that everyone will bring three logs to contribute to the fire, to make the most of everyone's hot stones. This ordinary oven, built by the Ambroisies' ancestors, is there for everyone, we pay a charge to use it, none of us can afford our own oven, even if it were allowed; so we all come with our dough. The oven was built at the edge of La Foye and is not located on anyone's land. On a given day old Magne spreads the word: tomorrow. It's never the same day, because the same day is too late, the dough needs time to rise. But tomorrow, yes, tomorrow there'll be bread, and Rose laughs at my excitement while she is getting out the leaven and the flour, and the day suddenly seems like a holiday. Bread is life.

So the leaven is on the table and we stare at it, our fascination mingled with respect. This leaven is older than we are. It has been regenerated hundreds of times, but it's also the same. Rose says it comes from her great-grandmother, perhaps even further back than that. Bread is infinite, it transcends us and our generations; it has witnessed us dying and being born, it has been there with us in joy and in hardship. People live and people die, their children replace them, and the leaven remains the same.

Rose has been slowly kneading the bread and I am dying to plunge my face into the rounds of dough where they sit proofing, swelling like dead hens, a smooth beige and gray gruel straining like a ripe fruit, the raw fragrance of the bread that doesn't yet exist. My head's spinning, Rose looks at me and smiles. There you go, she says. Long before Magne lights the first faggots on the floor of the oven we are clenching our jaws with expectation. In every house in La Foye, whether it's in the center of the village or on the farms spread out at the whim of the land and the fresh spring water, children are waiting. They're thinking about the little brown rolls that will bake next to the big ones, which will go to them first of all, a sort of treat that won't calm their hunger altogether but will make them so happy their hands will tremble; and every time it's the same, their bellies cry out before they can feast on the bread, elation is fidgeting, often the youngest children weep with emotion.

And the countryside may be gray, still rimed with frost, the next day when all the women from all the houses take their raw bread to the oven as soon as noon has passed, they are followed by a gaggle of laughing urchins as jittery as horseflies. On the underside of each loaf the women have traced a sign so they'll recognize them, their own sign, I mean, so there'll be no misunderstanding. Perhaps back in times of opulence those signs weren't necessary, but nowadays they have to keep an eye, they draw sticks and circles and crosses, each with its own meaning. They pay no attention to the fact that Magne knows his oven inside out, he has his own order, has grown so accustomed after nearly thirty years. He knows where, on the burning stones, to place each family's loaves, in his head he has assigned them their own spots, he could slide the loaves in with his eyes shut, and bring them out again, and hand them out without ever making the slightest mistake. Only the thing is, when you have barely enough to eat, you keep track. It's not even a calculation, it's instinctive. Life has hardened these women, these mothers, who'll look elsewhere while their children eat their hot rolls at the end of the baking, they'll look elsewhere, not to tell the fathers that they gave in, not to feel their stomachs rumbling, they'll take the crumbs and say that it's enough, for them.

Magne does at least three batches a day, the oven isn't big enough for a single batch. Often the women who have just come for their baked bread linger on. It's one day when they feel they have the right to stay and chat together—work can wait, it never goes away. In the evening they'll be wheeling home a hundred-weight of bread, so they can certainly sit for a moment and let the time go by, better still, take their own time, something people rarely experience around here. Around the oven there are stones and bits of wood, makeshift benches that have accumulated over the years, enough of them for everyone to sit until all the batches are done. Beyond the benches there are rows of neatly aligned wheelbarrows, where the women will load their loaves as Magne hands them out, with their lovely toasted crust, and the aroma that makes you feel faint.

Today is different. The women ask when the bread will be ready and they go back home to wait. It's still too cold for us to stand outside the bakery: only those whose bread is already in the oven stay; the ones whose loaves are next go to wait where they'll be sheltered from the wind. There's no chatting. No laughing. Most have only brought two logs instead of three, and flour is rationed: rather than eat their fill before dying of an empty stomach a month from now, the women would rather go hungry all the time, and they weigh the odds their families have of surviving if they cut down, and they have been cutting down since the end of the autumn. The bad seasons have spoiled the party. We're on the edge of the precipice and we all pretend that's not the case at all.

So we continue our roaming. I don't know where we find the energy to play in the glacial air of our countryside. The lack of food slows us down, yet something else is driving us, carrying us away, infallibly, erasing any adult-like gravity. Of Eugène's three sons Germain is the most serious, he has grown up. But the rest of us. Madelaine, Artaud, Mayeul and I . . . It's our way of telling death that it will not get us: we sing, we walk, we jump.

Dragging our feet. We don't care, since we can run. Our bodies, beneath our clothes, are dirty, no one undresses to sleep anymore, and Eugène's sons stink as much as me, I always stink, their necks are gray with grime, their jackets have that smell of sour skin, of sweat sticking in layers, at night we wrap ourselves in anything we can find to try to doze for a few hours. The hearth saves us even though by morning it's always cold; the first one up lights it again, we've gotten into the habit of living less than a stride away from the flames. Our world has shrunk. Narrow days, narrow spaces, narrow escapades. Only our hunger is huge. To forget about it, trick it, we drink, but we're sick of drinking, it makes us want to throw up, our stomachs cramp with spasms.

I spend more time lingering out of doors than the others. Madelaine often joins me and once again I find that closeness with her, our wild selves. The two of us head out to the forest, we are warriors, we fear nothing. We share this carefree attitude, something all-powerful, and yet we know very well that it's false, we are not invincible. We act as if. If we accept fear, we won't do anything anymore. We don't know terror, or only just. Sometimes Madelaine, in a dreamy voice, reminds me how it was the two of us, just the two of us, when we were carrying the dead deer back from the forest. The others ran away. But we. She pats me on the head. You and me, Bran.

That's our bond. Our shared bravery.

And besides, I would do anything for her.

We walk in the woods dusted with snow, and the sound of our breath is enough to bring peace. Each of us is looking to one side—a branch drooping with frost, leaves scattered by a wild boar, the sky gorged with sunlight or freezing rain—and we know that we're together. That's why we're not afraid. It gives us strength. If something happens, I think we'll react: anger, alarm, joy, desire or aggression, but no trembling. No terror. We're impervious to that feeling, we haven't grown up with it. And in that respect we're different from Eugène's sons, who have fear drilled into their bodies. Transmitted through their parents, and the parents of their parents. We have none of that.

We have courage.

We have rage.

As I said, we've stayed rather small. That's how you survive in extreme conditions: bigger people have greater need of food and warmth, so they're the first to die. More modest folk, like us—scrawny, tiny, wrinkled—are more sober in the space they take from the universe: they resist. When nature creates a difficult situation, it doesn't save the most handsome or the most imposing; it saves the strongest, and the strongest are those who have the fewest needs. Madelaine and I belong to that group. We do suffer from the cold, but less so than the others; we suffer from hunger but it doesn't stop us, our bodies are used to it, they're solid fortresses, our minds are scorched earth. And even if everyone has forgotten that Madelaine isn't Ambre's real daughter, because they are both strikingly beautiful, I can see what distinguishes them and sets them apart. Ambre is absolutely, but only, beautiful. What Madelaine has in addition is an elusive toughness. Ambre is a stone that can be spoiled, crumbled, broken; Madelaine is a diamond, nothing can cut into her.

And yet. I recall a merchant who set up his stall on the village square one day. He told us about a stone he'd had in his possession. A stone that was considered even rarer and more coveted, and worth more as well, because it had a particular feature: a crystallization, which made the stone fragile but at the same time gave it a remarkable brilliance. I can imagine just such a fissure in Madelaine. And it's not a weakness: it's a breach. Without it, the girl would be no more than coarse.

Only Ambre and Aelis have access to that heart of hers. When Madelaine hesitates, and doesn't show it—to show it would be to leave herself vulnerable, like an animal—she finds refuge in their company. It's often because of Germain. Because the eldest boy mistreats her. It's not that he's mean, but he's hard, harder with her than with his brothers. He senses that if they let Madelaine loose, no one will be able to control her. It's the same with restive animals, you have to hold them, firmly, tight, from the first to the last day, because otherwise all they'll be good for is to be slaughtered.

Madelaine helps out on Eugène's plot, to earn the vegetables that he'll give her. She'd like to do the work differently, her way, or in a different order, sideways when she's been told to go straight, and Germain has said no. Madelaine's eyes glow with anger. She asks him why. She explains what she would like to do. Germain shakes his head, No girl is going to—

Ah, ah, she cries, no girl is going to teach you how to bring home a deer, is that it?

They stare at each other. Madelaine is a whole head shorter than he is, weighs half what he weighs, and she's Mayeul's age. Yes, she is a girl. She will always be smaller and more delicate.

Germain looks down on her. He sends her away. He says, Get out. Go home. When she refuses, he shoves her. They've been known to grapple with each other, and we never know what to do, Artaud, Mayeul, and me, we wait for it to blow over. There's no point getting involved, it only makes things worse. I shouted once or twice, and all it got me was a clout from Germain. The quarrel always ends in the same way: Madelaine goes off, shouting insults, and then she falls silent, so we won't hear her sobs.

I go back with her. I'm walking silently behind her. I don't know if she realizes I'm here, or if she even cares, and I understand, we didn't stick up for her, didn't help her. We go back up to The Rises, I stop at Rose's, Madelaine is avoiding me. I watch as she runs toward the farms, toward the figure of Ambre or Aelis, whoever has seen her first, whoever calls to her, and she runs to them. Arms close around her and I lose her from sight. Their world is foreign to me; it's a world of women, where you have the right to feel despondent, a world that escapes me, I've never heard Eugène or his sons cry, or any of the men in La Foye. Madelaine cries with rage, with disappointment, with helplessness, they're tears all the same. In the sisters' arms she lets herself go. They kiss her, they calm her. They give her strength. We have nothing but blows and stubbornness to pull us up and make us strong. We observe that tiny little world women create among themselves, and we envy them, we too would like to be consoled when life overwhelms us, we hope for it with all our soul. But men get no comfort. They don't need it. We are devoured by our duty to power, we are forced to be invulnerable, to drive our fears and our despair deep into our guts. We are dying from the lack of love.

The following day, Madelaine comes back. Inside her, not a trace. She is rebuilt. She laughed with Aelis while sweeping the yard, she prepared supper with Ambre, she curled up and cuddled and found refuge, the darkness left her behind. The women's embraces dress her wounds, and by dawn the dark thoughts have been banished. I'd been walking with Eugène and his big horse; now I leave them and run to join her, whirl around her. She laughs and grabs me, she might say something mean, but she no longer thinks it, it's just to show me that she's forgiven me, that's her way. Life is open again.

The years pass slowly. That's a quality of this world, for it to be lazy, and leave us the time, as if we had something to complete, beyond struggling to survive, something to do before dying. So the years go by in long cycles, gloomy seasons, rain and frost take up too much space. The elders say it was worse before, and that it will come again, last time it was just like this: the earth gradually lost its balance, then poured out its anger onto humanity, two terrible years, and I saw the inhabitants of La Foye threaten the old people, their arms raised, telling them to be silent, birds of woe. Every day, we try our best to make them lie. We eat, even if the quality of the wheat is sometimes so poor that we're immediately hungry after we've supped, we don't want to listen to them, we want to live.

Madelaine is growing as slowly as the years, but now we've stopped saying she's our brother, she looks too much like a girl. She still follows us relentlessly, through the woods, through the fields, she teaches us a thing or two, that's not the problem; simply, we can't take her for a boy anymore. She has long hair, most often hidden under a light cap, when she hasn't mislaid it, and her features no longer have anything in common with Germain's or Mayeul's, which have grown thicker. Now we feel it, there are men, and there are women. But if being a woman means staying at the farm and looking after the house and the farm animals, Madelaine won't do it. She's not one of those girls. Ambre and Aelis pressure her gently, she is still young and time, yet again, will teach her. Madelaine balks. She doesn't want to. I know why, I know what being a woman here means. And in case I didn't know, Madelaine told me. It's happened to her, too. The most terrible thing is that if it hadn't been Madelaine, I wouldn't care. Until Madelaine came, I looked away. But when it happens to her for the first time, I cannot say that I feel nothing.

The day Léon touched her.

I didn't see it. She's the one who told me, right after it happened, her hands still trembling. We were sitting on a frozen slope, yet we didn't feel the cold, Madelaine's words were more heated and hateful than the chill of the earth. I understood that it was finished, never again would Léon be her father. He must never be called that again. Nothing good must ever be said about him—basically, it's not all that complicated.

And that reminded me of the evenings on feast days, when the villagers dance, and they drink, because there's no feast without some wine, bad plonk from the South that they buy, the one that's acidic but makes your head spin, that's all they want, to feel their heads spin. Wine warmth fatigue. And it's at moments like this that hands begin to wander, hands that think they can take liberties. Sometimes I feel ashamed. Hands always moving up, or down, never staying put. The women and girls laugh.

But later, they're not laughing.

It's not just Ambroisie-Son.

Maybe it's life that makes us like this. Life that's too harsh, testing us too often; bitterness and frustration accumulate inside. And so when one of us can become a master instead of a beggar, when there's a bit of power to be had, he doesn't hesitate. Weak with the strong and strong with the weak. We say they're perverts but they're simply men.

Madelaine thought it was strange, that hand slipping under her skirt one morning when Ambre was not there, when she'd gone to the village to barter a few vegetables. She said—that filthy disturbing gesture, with a whiff of the sordid, and she pushed Léon's hand aside abruptly, baring her sharp teeth like a little wild animal. Come on, said Léon, in a good-natured tone of voice, as if everything were obvious, as if he were talking to a half-tamed filly and all he had to do was say *Come on* for it to be all right, for him to try again.

You see, said Madelaine, struggling to breathe normally, you see, Bran, if he'd been angry, if he'd been brutal. But he wasn't. It all seemed so perfectly normal. What Madelaine needs is violence; in order to confront, she needs to clash head-on, and Léon was smiling. She thought he was smiling because nothing bad was happening. She was unsure of herself. Not for a moment did she suspect that Léon's smile meant he was sure.

That he could. That he would. Almost that it was his right. It was his breathing that changed everything. Madelaine froze, a little lost, and then that strange sensation that was like paralysis, she didn't dare move, was thinking as fast as she could.

But Léon's breathing.

Ragged. Rasping.

It reminded her of what she has sometimes heard at night when her parents think she's asleep, or don't care, and on their pallet at the other end of the room they lie on top of one another, making muted sounds. Instinctively she knows what it means. She's already seen dogs and pigs mating, outside in the yard, and the similarity is striking; no one talks about these things but they're in your blood, and when you see them, you know.

And so she leapt up.

She shouted like a howling cat—nothing comprehensible, she shouted, ears back and her teeth bared like a promise, and when Léon raised his voice and came back at her, she grabbed the knife that was next to the cookstove and stabbed the air in front of her.

Just then Madelaine laughed, a laugh that was too loud and full of fury, she very nearly slashed Léon's torso, because he wasn't expecting it. And he fell over, did Léon, and Madelaine is telling me this and demonstrating with her hands, a gesture of tumbling, he fell because of his bad leg, he tripped on the chair and there he was on the floor. In a split-second, Madelaine saw herself outside. She imagined climbing over Léon, running away into the countryside, going and looking for Ambre. Telling her everything. And then her initial reflex vanished and with the knife held between them, she knelt down next to the man still on the floor. She looked at him. He raised his gaze on her, his eyes full of anger, until he saw the blade. Madelaine was still observing him and there was a light in her, a glow of hatred. She waited. For the anger facing her to falter. For Léon to remember that she knew how to use that knife. She was the one who killed the chickens now, Ambre never liked doing it. This year she was also the one who'd cut the pig's jugular and carotid when they'd had the slaughter at Eugène's.

She didn't move until Léon saw.

The cold, implacable rage, he understood in a flash how, if he tried again, she would cut his throat, and quickly. He also realized that this was what she wanted: for him to understand, once and for all. For him to think about the death that would be his if ever. So he lowered his head. And I know he wasn't lowering it because he was sorry, but because he had failed. Madelaine was not afraid. She hadn't let him have his way. She's not normal.

But Léon is a bad sort, and he delivers his blows on the sly. I'm sure he was tempted to throw Madelaine out, to drive her from the house and erase the insult. He has no bond with the girl, no blood ties. He owes her nothing, she's a vagabond that Ambre took in, who eats from his table because he tolerates it, and maybe that's been going on for too long. The worst words, that's what he's capable of, this man with his petty mind, embittered by life, a bitterness that sees only faults and failings, and things upside down. With the help of bad wine, he has slipped to the bottom of his soul.

Léon gave way, too, because he knew that Ambre would never forgive him if he drove the girl out, he knew he couldn't. He probably doesn't even want to, he's grown attached to Madelaine, but he doesn't understand where the problem is. So his hands wandered, instinctively, by chance, because she is beginning to fill out, she's not a child anymore. Léon said to Madelaine, Where is the wrong? This has been going on for generations. He doesn't see why it would stop, that's all. And besides, Madelaine is not his daughter, it's not as if. It's different: as if he had a servant, a maid, someone in his house who isn't family, with servants you can do as you like.

Poor Léon, he'll never have a servant.

Madelaine looks at me. He had told her all that. His words were like a thrashing, she too lowered her head, stunned, that's what he wanted. A moment of inattention. Vigilance relaxed, anger surprised, and abruptly he reached out and grabbed the knife from her and threw it across the room. He laughed. And now? He pressed her against the wall.

The girl is no match for him. Her salvation is her vivacity, her quickness, but if you catch her she doesn't have the strength. She can't break loose, not without her knife, not without her hatchet. For that very reason she hates being a girl. She felt Léon's hand on her again. She shouted, she bit, in vain. He slapped her around the head so she would stop struggling.

She heard another shout, too. Behind Léon. A voice full of rage. Ambre was standing there, pale, she had picked up the poker from the hearth. She said, Let her go.

I look at Madelaine, who has fallen silent. I wait for the tears that are causing her eyes to shine, I wonder if they will flow, or if she'll wipe them away first. She seems so little, still such a child.

Her hands are lying on her hatchet. She says she will never let go of it again, ever, even to sleep.

That if it were not for Ambre.

Women, always.

I move closer to her, she puts her arms around me. Around my neck. She squeezes, hard. I nudge my head against hers and stop moving, I wait for it to pass, I take in her anger, her sorrow, I roll them up in a ball and throw them far away. We look at them in silence, winter casting a cold, yellow light.

At sixteen Germain obtained his land. He asked his father for it, he has the years and the strength, he has learned. That day, Eugène initially said nothing. He's always refused to work the Ambroisie fields. What he'd wanted was to go away. He was one of those who dreamt of leaving the Hinterland behind. He'd prepared himself, he'd imagined what it would be like, the farm would go to his elder brother Tébald, it was straightforward. And then Tébald died, like so many others, in an accident while plowing, and suddenly everything had changed: Eugène was now the eldest. The eldest does not leave. He knew this. He took a deep breath and accepted his destiny once again—but he would not work the Ambroisie land, where Tébald's blood had been spilt. He has never tilled their fields. At his farm he has to, but he will not work for them. Because he inherited the draft horse, Eugène turned to hauling lumber. The great commercial forests, beyond the Basilic, belong to other masters, not the Ambroisies. No one in La Foye can begin to imagine the rancor that runs deep in Eugène's chest; everyone else thinks it's an ordinary anger, the one all the men here feel, and which they've renounced for convenience's sake. And yet they feel it in their guts, as they watch the wheat growing, wheat that will not feed them, or not well enough, because half their yield will be taken from them; furthermore, taxes will be levied on those crops. The peasants feel they are working the land in vain, sowing with no hope of reward, either because the masters take too much, or because the weather is blighting the crops. In the end there is not even enough to feed their families. In any case the farms are too small to succeed; but if they did have more land they'd be incapable of farming it, the work is exhausting, they don't have the tools, or the money for the tools. No one knows how to break out of this vicious circle, and Eugène does not want to enter it. Where he goes, he is paid in cash, not grain. He is not at the mercy of the seasons, of drought or frost or disease.

And perhaps, Eugène simply likes his solitary work. Where he does his hauling he can hear the sound of the crosscut saws, and the woodcutters' axes, the trunks falling, cracking, voices shouting. It's his world. He is one of the only men who has a horse that pulls twice as fast as oxen, and he's better paid than if he farmed the land. This makes him proud. But it haunts him as well, because his privilege depends solely on Jéricho's strength and health, so he lavishes extensive care on him all year round.

And now Germain . . .

This occupation Eugène despises is what Germain wants.

He will have to ask Ambroisie-Father for land. Eugène has warned his eldest boy about the lease that runs even in famine years, and about the back-breaking work with hoe and spade, because oxen are rare here, there are only two in La Foye, and they belong to the family of Magne the baker, and he doesn't lend them out. There is also the climate, which has become harsher—the old folk still alive say the land produces less nowadays than when they were young, the crops multiply the seed by three instead of by five, when the frost or rot doesn't get to everything. And yet, Germain has made up his mind, and Eugène gives up. They have only one horse for all of them, they cannot haul more than they already do, there's no point in all of them going to the forest if the sons don't want to be woodcutters. Germain has been helping in the fields for years, hiring himself out as a farmhand: he loves the land. He wants his own. He will do it with Artaud. The two of them will be indefatigable, and besides, it will give them a little leeway, a little security, too, if something were to happen to the horse. Eugène shakes his head, Germain is right, but is he prepared to run from one plot to the next—the plots are small and scattered, and to obtain five hectares, you need a dozen of them. Germain nods, he knows all that, he agrees, he will sprint from one end of his land to the other.

He acquires his censives in the middle of winter, too late for sowing, he'll have to wait patiently for the spring wheat, buckwheat, or oats. In the meantime, Germain must prepare the land, if it isn't too hard with frost; he has to think about rotating, too, he knows that folk here plant a year of autumn cereal, a year of spring cereal, and the third year the ground lies fallow. Of the five hectares he's received, he will, therefore, cultivate only slightly more than three a year, it already seems a lot, and yet it wouldn't even provide enough to eat if he were alone; his head is spinning, there are too many things to think about. Eugène gives him advice, memories from the time when his own parents worked the land. They could keep a small plot of alfalfa for Jéricho's fodder, it would save them having to buy it, they would gain. For the rest: grain, grain, and more grain. That's what wealth is, what ensures bellies will be filled. Grain that can be made into bread as much as possible, wheat and rye, with the others they'll have to mix the flours, but buckwheat doesn't need much, it's a sure asset, Germain dreams of it at night, he sleeps badly, the land is being plowed in his head.

Three times, said Eugène.

Three times over the fields that will produce the grain must be plowed, with hoe and spade, always, you might as well say with the strength of your arms and your back, to loosen the soil, make it welcoming, it's like their bedding at night, if Ambre and Aelis don't shake it and plump it and air it out, it gets as hard as wood.

Germain will do it.

And so, as soon as the days allow it, he and Artaud begin

to turn over his fields. They leave at the same time as Eugène, when day is breaking; soon they part ways, the father heading west toward the Basilic and the forests, and the boys north and east where they have their plots at the edge of the younger woods. They go by rain or wind or shine; only hard frost stops them, when their implements recoil from the earth's carapace. Germain has bought implements on credit from the smithy for working the earth, not very many to be honest, and he will pay at the first harvest. He adds them to the spades and hoes that were his late grandparents', which they take with them in the wheelbarrow: they won't need to go home if a handle breaks or blade gets twisted.

Mayeul and Madelaine often go with them when they're working the land at the edge of the oak forest. The younger siblings lead the two pigs to the woodland pasture and collect wood. They keep an eye on their older siblings as they labor, huffing and puffing amid the straight furrows; to them the effort seems colossal, and magnificent. When all four pause at the Angelus to share their bread, Germain laughs and sits down, his features drawn with fatigue. He talks about the seeds to be sown, the plants that will sprout like magic beans—he's planned cereal for two thirds of the crops, and legumes for the rest, broad beans and peas with their abundant yield, far more resistant, if the season proves difficult. He speaks of the first harvest as if it were a treasure and yet it is a long way off, for the moments the ground is a mass of empty clods. Around the broken bread, four pairs of eyes shine.

Before long, Madelaine and Mayeul refuse to tend the swine: there's better work to be done in the fields. But the pigs cannot keep themselves, and Aelis and Eugène say no. This is what families are for, too, sharing out the chores, to each their own burden, they themselves were raised this way, first the fowl and the little woods, when they were four or five, then the chores getting bigger and bigger as the years went by; the fields will be for later. It's just that Madelaine doesn't agree. She discusses. She argues. One morning she explains that she and Mayeul will bring back more, and better, by helping their siblings than by running behind the pigs, this stupid job that anyone can do and which the villagers usually assign to half-witted children, but she and Artaud are not simpletons, they deserve real work. Aelis sends her packing. So Madelaine goes off without the pigs. She leaves Mayeul there, along with her aunt and the animals. She goes home. Ambre is surprised to see her back already: Madelaine says she won't be a pig keeper any more, she wants Léon's tools to go and join Germain and Artaud, she rummages in the barn. When at the hour of the Angelus Mayeul comes along the fields with his pigs, he sees all three of them, his older brothers and his cousin, bent over the earth, dirty sweat darkening their faces. Madelaine calls to him. He shouts that he can't come, because of the pigs, and because of her, too, and she shrugs. Leave them! she cries. Mayeul hesitates, and then the temptation is too great, he runs over to them. In the beginning, the pigs paw at the ground, and turn around them; but after a while they wander off. Mayeul keeps an eye on them, ill at ease, they're not just animals, they are their food, their subsistence, their survival. Finally they disappear, and he can't stand it anymore: he runs off in pursuit. Germain mocks him, calls him chicken-livered, his words ringing in the woods all around. That evening when he gets home, Mayeul tosses his cape and his stick into a corner of the room, without a word, looking sullen. When Eugène asks what's wrong, Artaud tells him. Their father begins to laugh. Madelaine is at it again, he thinks, but he likes that way of hers, adamant, wanting to work ever harder; if the girl refused to help out, it would irritate him far more. Well then, he says, I was wrong.

The next day Aelis takes on a boy from the village who is about eight years old. In exchange for bread at noon and a ration in the evening before he goes home, the boy helps out as her sons have done until now, in the farmyard and the vegetable garden, with the pigs, with all the chores she gives him, unsparingly, and which he carries out without a word, to earn his pittance. It's customary in the village to hire each other's children, to train them, and moreover it means one less mouth to feed for those families that are even poorer. Aelis lets Mayeul go, Ambre lets Madelaine go, and we all head for Germain's fields. We always go together, a slow-footed clan, softened by exhaustion. Germain and Artaud take turns pushing the wheelbarrow with the tools. At work, Madelaine and Mayeul are not spared. When they stumble with fatigue at the end of the day, Germain sits one of them in the cart and wheels them home, dozing to the bumps in the road, hardly eating before collapsing until the following dawn, until the moment a brother or mother wakes him and it's time again to run along the path leading to the fields. As the weeks go by, despite the bad weather, the earth is turned over, scraped, raked. Germain has kept two fallow plots where he is letting a villager's sheep graze in exchange for manure. The soil is poor, eager for manure, which is never available in sufficient quantity. Everything's hard, and takes a long time, says Mayeul, dismay in his voice. They have to accommodate nature, learn patience, accept that, sometimes, everything will be destroyed. Above all, they have to start again: start working, turning over the earth, sowing, weeding, reaping. The cycle is round and never-ending. It is a source of exhaustion but also of wonder, because unlike mankind, nature always makes a fresh start, even badly, even just a little. Meanwhile, winter freezes our noses and ears, and we can only imagine what our land will be like once it's been planted and the grain has begun to grow. For now it looks like a huge empty field, as if moles had ransacked it, we find it hard to picture it full and green. We think about the bad years in the past, the ones that froze half the seeds, or rotted them, or dried them on the stalk. Germain claps his hands and we give a start. We are there. We return to work, we forget that we might fail.

It is a cold, white day, yet another, and Germain has given up on going to the fields for a week now. In the morning he and Artaud leave with Eugène, in the forests they need help with the wood, the wood they cut up right there and arrange in long low piles ready to be carted away. Mayeul, Madelaine, and I tease Aelis's hired boy as he runs from one chore to the next around the farm. Perhaps we'll go with him when he takes out the pig, the one remaining pig, since according to tradition the other one was eaten at Christmas: one little pig in December, and the other, which will have grown to perhaps two hundred-weights or more, in February. What a thrill, at the end of every summer, the day Eugène brings home the piglets he's bought from the Constant farm, where they have three sows. Half the village goes to the Constant farm because their stud boar gives them big, meaty porkers, and they're worth the few coins Eugène and Léon put on the table, when Léon doesn't barter a pair of new clogs for a little pig, no one has had any call for complaint, the meat will be good. I remember the three feast days when the men held the last pig-killing in the village, they slaughtered six animals one by one that week, one every morning, three in the little village, and three on the farms. One day to kill and make the blood sausages, one day for the meat and ham, one day for the sausages with made with the offal. Afterwards there's the salting and drying. There's an impression of happiness. Ambre and Aelis took chunks of meat to Rose, it seems long ago now, there's no more smell of meat in our house, just a bit of lard hanging by the fireplace, from which Rose cuts parsimoniously.

But Madelaine couldn't care less about the pigs, she's not interested in keeping them anymore, now that we've grown. Now that we're true peasants, with our land, since we've appropriated Germain's fields for ourselves. And so because we're already bored, we run into the woods. We go a long way. We don't cry out, we're not playing, as if we too had become adults by acquiring territory. For the first time I notice how hollow-cheeked Madelaine has become, how careworn her expression is. She looks like a young woman, not a little girl. This fatigue troubles me less when I see it in Eugène's sons, perhaps because they're men. We know what men are like when they're exhausted: coarse, uncouth. But girls. I still hope there'll be some roundness, some sweetness, some beauty that even poverty cannot erase. Girls are not made to have dark circles around their eyes, or furrows in their cheeks, they shouldn't have these old women's hands and bent backs. Madelaine is maybe twelve or thirteen years old, and she's a thousand years old. Worn down by life, by ordinary hunger, by the demands life makes of us simply to go on. Bit by bit La Foye has been losing people. Two old men and a child have died since autumn, you hardly notice, and yet, people are dying too early, it seems to me that something is hurtling toward us. We are paying for the accumulation of the lean years, at the time we paid no attention, there were no terrible disasters like ten years earlier, it's just that there's been too little for too long. The men remain valiant, then drop dead all of a sudden. Madelaine would make fun of me if she knew my thoughts, but she's like me, like us, on a rope so threadbare that the sigh of a child could cause it to snap. Only Artaud takes care of her, Artaud and the twins, who are still so sweet with her, a sweetness we all envy but there's no bitterness. Sometimes Madelaine asks Ambre who is her favorite of them all, and Ambre exclaims, hugs her with a laugh and says, It's you of course. Aelis, next to them, joins their embrace. She says, You're my favorite, too, and I hear them laugh; the sons act as if it were nothing, or, on the contrary, they cry out and make fun of them, those women with their feelings all the time, if only they could eat those feelings, there'd be no hunger, no famine.

So we're walking, and listening, Madelaine and I, in the cold of winter, with this fog that doesn't want to lift. We keep on going, our ears burning, even if we have to listen out for a bird or the scurrying of rodents. We look for any tracks of game, until we end up having visions.

And suddenly I'm the one who hears.

I've come to a halt and Madelaine is observing me. I have the best hearing of all of us, and now I've picked up a sound carried on the wind. Her gaze is questioning, we're silent. It's the hunters, I know at once. It's the Ambroisies. And yet I don't move, I listen. We should have left right away, but I stand there motionless, undecided, the time we will wish we'd had, after.

Bran?

I turn my head to Madelaine. Now she too can hear the muffled sound of the horses in the snow, the men's shouts, encouraging the dogs.

The dogs.

We both whip around. We don't have much energy, but we get out of there fast, back to the heart of the woods, where we have hiding places, where we'll be in with a chance. We don't make it. The barking is getting closer, coming too quickly, and Madelaine growls, keeping her voice low, They think we're game for them, they're hunting us. I look behind us, and I could run faster, I could get away, but only if I leave Madelaine and I can't conceive of it. So I push her and we set off again, breathless, lungs freezing, hearts burning. I'd rather die in flight than in the fangs of the huge German pointers, and I can hear the hunters calling them back, telling them off, I can picture the handlers taking them on the leash, our heartbeats are pounding in our ears like drums, deafening.

This way, says Madelaine. I don't recognize her croaking voice.

We're still running. The bare trees protect us for a few minutes, a few more seconds. That's not what we're thinking of, we're thinking only of reaching the houses, our odds of getting there, we're not thinking of defeat. All our spirit, all our soul aiming for The Rises.

We run.

The sound of our steps on the snow-covered leaves, the scrape when we stumble. Madelaine, her mouth gasping for a little air for her saturated lungs.

We run.

My eyes are streaming with cold. I can feel my heart leaping under my ribs, rising in my throat. My body is gone, there are limbs and organs and everything is dislocated with the effects of frost, flight, my ragged breathing.

And I stop. Madelaine stops likewise, two steps in front of me. We feel the vibration. Madelaine doesn't have time to understand, she's only human, but I do. The image is printed upon my mind in a flash.

And because I know that Madelaine can't get away, because I know she hasn't yet identified the sound of a crossbow the moment the bolt is shot, and that we have a fraction of a second before we are mortally hit, I throw myself forward. The muscles in my paws tear with the effort, my body is propelled like a ball of fire. The moment I jump in front of her, protecting her with my entire body, the arrow enters, right in my side. There is pain. Immense, searing. The girl cries out, her hands in my blood-spotted fur as I fall into the snow. But it all happens too quickly. My mouth wide open, I take in a lungful of air, a lungful of fog, perhaps. Madelaine cries my name. And then everything fades.

Three

Winter has overlooked Madelaine's sorrow. As with humans, the death of the dog has become invisible. There's no time, no strength. More and more often, thoughts are clouded by the need to find some tiny thing to eat every day; it has the bitterness and sharpness of a dagger turning in flesh, the sensation is physical, terribly real, so much so that when someone has died, they are hardly mourned. Mourning eats away that little bit more at the vitality that is so sorely lacking. Alongside the absence of the dead, there is the relief of sharing less of the food rations; there are fewer folk around the fire. So no one can really understand why Madelaine is so sad about her dog, when so many humans have already succumbed. She beats her chest. She says, *my* dog. Eugène's sons give a shrug. For them it was just an animal. Madelaine came to blows with Germain.

In the days that followed, Artaud softened toward her. It's strange how, without realizing it, he is now walking in the dog's tracks. When they're on their way home from the fields and there's still some daylight to be spent in the woods, he goes with Madelaine. He sits beside her. Sometimes he says nothing. He is there. The girl is totally absorbed by the forest, not really paying attention to him. Time is gathered in and Artaud becomes a regular presence, a bit like the crickets in summer—when you go outside, you don't expect them, you don't think about them, but as soon as you hear them you know everything is as it should be. Madelaine and Artaud exchange a few words, in the beginning it was to carp about Germain, or to speak about the dog's absence and their hatred of the Ambroisies, and then they let it go, now they look out at the world. Artaud has changed, as they all have, he has grown into a body subjected to hunger, gnarly, muscular from want. And despite the weariness, he has retained his handsome features; Madelaine sometimes gazes at him when he's working side by side with Germain, she compares them, to the detriment of the older brother, it makes her smile. Artaud is taciturn. On days when Madelaine hears his voice she savors its low, gentle timbre, the words not barking orders. The middle son is seeking where to position himself between Germain's strength and Mayeul's cheerfulness. While he is still fascinated by his older brother, he is also more circumspect. He knows that Germain does not do everything well. His demands are disproportionate, and he is hard, forcing the others to comply, like it or not. With Madelaine, Artaud can escape. Until now the place was taken, and he thinks, puzzled, that the girl preferred the company of her dog; or maybe he, Artaud, was the one who remained aloof, on his own. Now he runs to catch up with her. Once or twice he has taken her hand. He is filled with a strange, warm sensation in his chest.

Madelaine suppresses her sadness and anger. They are buried deep inside her, she has understood that she couldn't speak about the dog, not like that, not as if he were better than a human. And it's true that the endless winter has obliged her to turn to other things: Léon doesn't go out much, doesn't work much, doesn't bring home much. Food is getting scarce. If Eugène hadn't given Madelaine more than her due from the herbs in the garden, if he hadn't shared his flour because Aelis insisted, in the name of her sister, at the second farm on The Rises they would be starving.

And it's not only the frost, because it doesn't freeze for months on end; it's simply the cold, and the damp, one of those combinations that makes the tree branches crack, and shatters any pots left outside. On those days, Madelaine and Eugène's sons stay indoors, glued to the fireplace to dry and warm their bodies that are as cold as the air, they only go out when it cannot be helped. There is already too much that cannot be helped, they have to run through the forest collecting firewood, they are depleting their stocks, the wood is damp, stored in a corner to dry out, the fire smokes until it catches, water hisses from the logs. This type of fire does not heat well, initially emitting its own chill; you could put your hands on the wood, you wouldn't get burned.

Sometimes Eugène takes Madelaine with him to the other side of the Basilic. Her skill with the hatchet and her stamina at work have proved precious when it comes to delimbing, for preparing the kindling. So while Eugène is leading the horse to the hauling site, the girl is chopping, cutting, sectioning, then bundling the branches she piles at the edge of the path. She says it's not very different from the wheat she'd cut with a sickle and bound in sheaves at the end of the summer. She's glad to be using her hatchet again, to forget the farmland for a while, even if Artaud is glum when he sees her leaving with his father and the big horse. Eugène smiles, calling Madelaine *my youngest son*. It's not often that Eugène smiles, and Madelaine is jubilant when she tells her mother. Léon pretends not to hear.

But at last winter is on its way out. They'd begun to lose faith that spring would ever come, as if it could disappear. Like everyone, Eugène's sons and Madelaine hurry to the fields. The tension and teasing, the hierarchy among them, all vanish in a morning, effaced by the softness of the air and the milky blue sky stretching above them. All swept away by hope, with the insane joy of putting their bodies to good use again. They count the months. Germain says they will thresh the wheat soon after the harvest, to have grain to grind, four or five months from now; they can picture it already.

From daybreak to dusk the cousins work together on

Germain's land. Among themselves they have re-created the same silent alliance as at the beginning of winter, when they were preparing the land. Alone, they would have accomplished nothing, but now that they've understood that, by uniting, they've made everything possible, they've become a clan. It's not just the distribution of chores that has come to them naturally, each according to their strength and talent—that's something others do, too. It's something to do with surpassing themselves, something they have no words for. If they knew how to say it, they would talk about love—family love, blood love, loyalty and giving, all of which they can feel in their guts and which lifts their spirits when exhaustion has left them low—the love that makes them rush to help whoever has stumbled. The bond they feel is incredibly strong, yet they cannot express it, it's inside them, written in their flesh, this bond that might even be as strong as that of a mother protecting her child. Every evening Eugène's sons endure a separation from Madelaine when she returns to her house—it's not painful, rather, it's a strange physical sensation, as if a part of the three sons were leaving with her and floating in the air between the two farms, a pang in their bellies, a tightness in their chests. The burst of enthusiasm they have in the morning when they meet up again is proof of what they have missed, of the subtle void, the restlessness of the nights when they no longer form their little group. Energy radiates through them as they find their place in the row, striding along the path, Mayeul to the left, then Madelaine, then Germain pushing the wheelbarrow with the tools, it's always Germain who takes the wheelbarrow first; finally Artaud on the right. Mayeul is taller than Madelaine even though they're the same age. Germain surpasses all of them in height but Artaud is catching up, next year he'll be the easiest to see from afar. They are solid and thin like the trunks of the old walnut trees that border some of the bean fields. And so along they go, of unequal height, swinging together down the path—that is what matters: together. When the peasants see them in the distance they call them the gang of four. That's how they recognize them.

Of course there's also tiredness and moodiness. Quite often Germain sends one of the younger ones back to The Rises for one reason or another. Often it's to defuse a confrontation between them, an outburst of anger or pain. Mayeul continues to chatter like a magpie, Artaud reproaches him, says he is prattling to the detriment of his work. Madelaine gets involved to defend her cousin, she says he's working his fingers to the bone, Germain stops them, reasons with them; if he doesn't manage to make them see reason, he separates them. There are also times when he sends the youngest two back to the farms to spare them, if he sees them staggering in the furrows, the heat making them dizzy or the cold freezing their fingers and jaws. He tells them there's a knife he's forgotten, or a bag, he asks for a tool that won't even be used. Madelaine or Mayeul or both of them head off, their gazes lowered, hesitating between the relief of a moment's respite and the humiliation of a provisional excommunication; at such moments they understand the strength of their clan, the fissure that appears whenever they are divided. When they return, nothing is said. Backs bent, they resume their place and go on working, there are no words between them, only eyes creasing in a smile, Artaud nudges his little cousin, Go on, they take their spades and dig the rows together, tomorrow they will sow.

The first year is generous. It must be a stroke of luck, but they welcome it with laughter, they take everything, the wheat slides between their fingers. Germain—through his father, because he is not yet of age—has paid the dues on his land, and shares the crops and the harvest: half for himself, the other half split among the four of them, as it should be, unequally, because Mayeul and Madelaine don't put in as much work as the older boys, despite the girl's surprising vigor. But they agreed on it beforehand, and no one objects. Besides, there's so little left, most of the grain goes to paying for the land and for the workers who came at harvest-time, and for reimbursing the tools. Still, they have threshed the wheat, the gang of four, and despite the dust and the pain in their arms from the flail, they are nothing but joy: at last something has been accomplished. Germain takes the surplus to be milled, and they share the sacks of flour. The day the sons show their mother the cart full of sacks, and Madelaine pushes the wheelbarrow home with her part (it takes her three trips, with Artaud's help), that day feels like a holiday. A perpetual holiday, or so you believe at that age—once it's begun, everything will be all right. A holiday that will bring better things, growing from year to year, and the gang of four begin to dream of a life where their back-breaking work will at last allow them to live.

Madelaine also takes a sack of flour to Rose. They don't see each other often, the girl gazes from a distance at the woman who seems old to her now, and the ties the dog had woven between them are gone; but she has never forgotten that it was Rose who found her, and took her in, and fed her. She owes her return to the world to Rose, and does not know how to express it, is hardly aware of it, simply that the emotion is still there when she sees her again, an upsurge that makes her want to embrace her, so sometimes she does and Rose laughs as she closes her arms around her. Madelaine, like Ambre and Aelis when they are together, steals time to be with Rose. She helps her a little in the garden. And when age begins painfully twisting the old woman's fingers, preventing her from making delicate gestures, Madelaine enters into the fascinating world of plants. Initially she merely fills little jars with ointment—leaves reduced to powder, unfamiliar concoctions that have been macerating. But this, too, she wants to understand. So Rose begins to explain. Madelaine discovers how very ignorant she is, and not just she alone: her parents, too, her uncle and aunt, her cousins. In the entire village, only Rose has knowledge. The way Madelaine views her changes radically. Rose is not simply an aging woman who needs her, or others, to help with bringing in the firewood or turning over the earth; Madelaine is the one who needs Rose. To learn. This is very different from sowing, weeding, reaping. This time, she has to use her mind. She emerges from her lessons feeling elated, despairing, headachy. She will never manage to learn everything, to keep it all in her head. It takes at least ten years, Rose whispered to her, and they remain silent, they do not want to admit that Rose doesn't have ten years. They busy themselves with the most everyday ointments. Madelaine is lively, explosive. She works quickly, understands quickly, too quickly. Often she pours a little too much, or spills a little, or heats something more than she should, or forgets an ingredient. Rose corrects her, tirelessly, teaches her patience and slowness. Sometimes she makes her sit down between two operations, makes her recite the steps she has just performed and list those to come. The girl complies, with good grace, and she makes progress, too, but now and then she comes up against something and her temper immediately gains the upper hand. She runs out of the house, shouting that she's stupid, and doesn't come back for three days. Besides, it's her duty to work in the fields, to help around the house; she hasn't told the others what she's doing at Rose's. It's between her and Rose. Sometimes when she comes home Ambre sniffs her and says, You smell like aromatic herbs. Madelaine replies with a shrug. It's from Rose's place. At Rose's it smells like plants.

At the end of the summer the gang of four sow Germain's plots with autumn wheat. The weather is mild and humid, exactly as they hoped, the soil is loose, offering no resistance when the tools break its surface. It's like their first harvest: it's dangerous, everything coming so easily—and yet it's not easy, Germain tells himself, his chapped hands bleeding; he puts pork fat on them, the chapping doesn't heal. It's dangerous because they're getting used to finding something filling on the table almost every day. Eugène and Léon told them about the terrible years at the end of the last century; the gang of four are too young to remember, but hunger is written in their bellies, they know nothing else. It was during those two years of great famine that their grandparents died, and, in all probability, Madelaine's parents, too, before the new seasons brought some mercy. But the fathers don't believe in good fortune, they don't trust it. They try to eat sparingly, as if they didn't want to be caught out when hardship returns; sometimes they remove the bread, saying it's for tomorrow, they count Germain's peas and beans and stow entire sackfuls in the loft. They are stockpiling. When the children shout, and exclaim that the lofts are infested with insects and that the flour and beans will be ruined, they don't listen. They know. There is no such thing as abundance in this country relentlessly despoiled by war and taxes and climate. Bad flour can be eaten all the same, it's better than nothing, they've known famine, it has marked them. Germain eventually yields to their caution, fear is contagious. He looks at his fields with a new apprehension, overcome by thoughts he's never had. He's angry with Eugène for instilling this fear in him; he's alarmed to think that his parents' terror might contaminate his soil, that their words might turn to prophecies, or curses. His dream clashes with their resignation and rebels, too late, everything has been damaged. He too frowns, looking out at the black earth, turned and sown. What if they're right. What if hope is a vain thing.

And yet everything proceeds counter to their fears and predictions, because the winter spares them, and the spring once again makes the wheat ripen. It's hot in the month of April, then in the beginning of May, and the stems have come up, tall and strong, a tender green that makes you want to eat them straight from the ground. The earth was warm very early, welcoming, comfortable. It rains, too, and the soil is full of life. In the village they have all sown, they all laugh to see the fine days and the plants coming up and growing, week after week.

It is too warm, yes.

Germain has a premonition that the weather will not hold, but perhaps this is his father's influence on his mind, he doesn't know anymore. No one knows. There is just this summery month of May and at the moment, no indication that a few days later, a northeast wind will rise to shake off its winter, belatedly, and that it will freeze the countryside four nights in a row, burning everything in its path, the buds and the flowers on the fruit trees, and the young crops in the fields. They look, terrified to see that what was prematurely green is now turning brown and withering on the stem, and nothing will be saved, they will have to rely on the seeds kept by, to try and replant, in haste, there won't be enough, this coming summer will be mediocre, ruining the harvests.

In July, as in August, the men watch the sky for the fine dry weeks that will allow them to cut the wheat and gather it in, to make the hay into stacks, in a word, to ensure that during the cold season they will be sheltered from hunger, and their animals, too: they wait in vain. They end up bringing in a meager harvest, ruined by humidity. The gang of four too were obliged to cut the wheat during a partial drizzle, the season was turning late, everything was drenched, by September they had to resign themselves. Germain has ordered them to spread the grain as widely as possible in the lofts so that the moisture will evaporate; as soon as he finds it is dry enough, he will take it to the mill. And no one knows whether the flour will keep or will be sticky and turn moldy, they have not sealed the sacks, they hope and pray in silence, all in their own way, whenever one of them goes to check on the state of the reserves and plunges his arm into the flour. It has to come out white, powdery, light. They have been wondering what they will do if it begins to rot. Bread, right away, says Germain. While there's still time. We'll pay to have the oven to ourselves, dozens and dozens of loaves, which we'll try to keep, they'll be hard, we'll soak them. Provided they don't go moldy. None of them wants to see this happen, there is too much at stake.

Perhaps the sky hears them—the flour doesn't spoil. There's just not enough. They eat more cautiously, autumn comes early, they try to sow some winter wheat. Supplies dwindle more quickly than expected and October, in turn, is still wet. It rains thirty-eight days in a row. The soil is gorged with water, withering half the grain. In places, where rivulets wind along the edge of the fields, seeds are being emptied into ruts and are borne away by the flooding rain. The gang of four straggle home from the fields, soaked through, ragged, backs broken. Not long thereafter they stop going every morning: there's nothing to be done. The sparsely scattered crops are rotting, the stems going moldy before they can even grow. The men from the village whom the gang of four encounter are as despondent as they are, don't know what to do with their hands and arms; to give themselves a purpose, they resort to wood, to the multiple little things of everyday life in their houses and barns. But the waiting is long, the rain returns incessantly, the earth has no time to breathe, no time to absorb a downpour before the next one is already there. Christmas comes and goes without their having been able to go back to the fields. The prospect of a bad season becomes terrifying.

And all at once, a new winter takes them without warning.

During the night of January 6, flows of polar air that had begun to freeze the countryside the night before send temperatures plummeting to well below freezing. The glacial wind exacerbates the sensation of cold that now seizes man and beast. They are run through by cold, indescribably; they feel as if they have been frozen to the bone: their clothing serves no purpose, so deeply does the air penetrate, everywhere, bruising flesh that freezes from within. Even breath must be taken in little gasps not to burn sinuses and throat. Madelaine's fingers are numb and she blows on them, under the illusion that this will warm them; she can't feel them anymore, she's afraid they'll fall off. Yet again they leave the fields behind.

They wait patiently for two days before returning to their devastated crops, taking turns walking two in the lead in front, and the other two following, eyes closed, to avoid the frost that glues their eyelids shut and makes them weep tears of ice. Around their heads they've wrapped cloth torn from their shirts. The chill beats against their temples and attacks their ears with a whistling that drills into the hollows in their skulls. Any patch of skin not covered—on the verge of coming to shreds. Never before have they been confronted with air that brings such cold; never before have they thought they could die from the weather, but that day they all believe it, struck by the violence of the blizzard, by their solitude in a world that is swathed in opaque white veils, and their vision reaches no farther than a few feet.

In the fields, it was a calamity foretold: all the shoots that had survived the rain have frozen. The ground hardened so quickly that walking on it no longer crushes the clumps of earth. They go home, shivering, and Germain says they will have to count their sacks of flour; one after the other they register the bad summer and the destruction of their autumn crops, the spring will yield nothing, he says the granaries will soon be empty, their fathers had been right, they won't make it through the winter, this time, the hunger that has always had its grip on them will kill them.

The winter brings them to their knees. Entire weeks go by, and the earth does not thaw, the ground is as hard as a rock grown over the world. Every morning, men break their ankles on frozen tufts of grass. They've had to lay planks over the tops of wells, for fear the water too will freeze. Madelaine and Artaud go down to the Basilic one day; they have never seen its banks hemmed in the way they are now. The ice embraces the river's edge then ventures out for six feet or more, until the current stops it. They hesitate to step out onto the ice to check the thickness. They don't dare. The air is so cold they have difficulty breathing.

The wave of frost does not let up. There are nights Madelaine wakes up shivering, when ordinarily she's not afraid of cold temperatures. She hears the wind through the gaps in the windows, although they are closed with double shutters, and she knows that something exceptional is happening. Something that will last until springtime, fracturing January with unprecedented temperatures; the trees stay white with frost day after day, the walls of houses spit out cold air even when the fireplaces are fed, relentlessly. Mayeul and Madelaine are in charge of the firewood, it's still damp, but they need it. At Eugène's, they all sleep in their parents' big bed to share a bit of warmth. Ambre and Léon call to Madelaine but she refuses to join them under the blankets, preferring to curl up at the far side of the room with the dogs they've brought indoors, which lie on the warm stone of the hearth. Madelaine runs her fingers through their fur. Sometimes she thinks of Bran, then banishes the image of the big dog, shot through with the arrow of a crossbow. It's hard to fall asleep when the cold bites; frozen hands and feet give her no respite, causing her to shiver instinctively, disturbing her body and her mind, which won't fall silent, won't stop lamenting and sniveling about how cold it is, even inside the house where, sometimes, in a corner, the surface of the water in a jug has frozen over.

Every night, Madelaine tells herself that it's another night gained on all the cold nights to come, although every morning when she joins her cousins, with their long pale faces, she feels more vulnerable. She goes to Rose's practically every day, as much to continue her slow apprenticeship as to make sure the old woman is still alive. Rose's words and gestures seem dull, as if they too have been trapped by the frost, frozen in her head. There are mornings when Rose can't come out with what she wants. Madelaine makes sure there's some hot soup on the fire, she chats for a moment, looks at the little jars filled with balm. To bring the moment to life, she asks about this jar or that, what it's used for and what the main plant is, in the springtime where will they go for betony, and where for swallowwort. She would like to be with Rose then, she would like to know the places, all the places smell of the secret—where to go for mushrooms, for berries, for plants. Rose nods, but doesn't always answer. Madelaine puts wood in the fireplace and goes away again, never entirely reassured.

On the way from Rose's farm to hers, she sometimes comes upon a small creature that has frozen all at once, lying there stiff in the white countryside, a creature that thought it would find a little something to eat in the proximity of the houses: a little rodent, its eyes still full of surprise, or a ruffled bird, and even cats that had come out to hunt and gone farther than they should have. Sometimes she takes it home to Ambre, they hesitate to eat it, and then hunger wins out and Ambre skins the cat as if it were a hare, hanging it from a pole, its hide pulled over its head. In the soup, no one can tell the difference.

The sun has not shown its face in weeks, the days are a damp gray that accentuates the feeling of cold. All it takes is a little wind, sometimes just a breeze, to turn their faces and hands to ice. The grass is as if melted beneath the frost; when Madelaine walks outside, it cracks to her step, cracks beneath her fingers when she touches a tree or a plant, there is nothing she can take hold of without breaking it; everything that is alive, whether with sap or with blood, becomes, in the extreme cold, more fragile than glass. One day she finds a shrew, caught by the night, completely stiff. She picks it up, starts to remove a few twigs that are stuck to its fur, and the little animal snaps in two, leaving her with the top of its body in one hand and the bottom in the other. The interior is red but the blood doesn't even flow, as frozen as the bones projecting whitely along its spine. Madelaine stands there for a moment looking at the shrew as if she were trying to work something out; then she puts the two halves one on the other and places it back on the ground, in the same position in which she found it. She doesn't want to eat that creature. And in any case, the shrew is too small, too thin as well, just like the humans. Madelaine leaves it at the edge of the path.

Branches overcome by frost crack and fall to the ground with a sound of dead wood, setting the rhythm to their days. Everything is dying. From the village to The Rises, they know they cannot get away, no matter how they struggle, they won't all make it. In La Foye, four old people and three more children have died, they can't stand up to the cold when there's nothing left to eat. The earth has frozen too hard, and the men have had to hoist the corpses wrapped in cloth into the branches of tall trees to keep them out of reach of predators, until the thaw, until they can bury them. They make strange iced fruits overhead when the living wander through the forest in search of firewood or in hopes of bringing back a dead animal; the corpses cast long shadows that sway slowly, reflected on the ground when the wind blows out of the northeast. The dead children make smaller bundles; under normal circumstances it is old folk who are hoisted up into the trees. It's not normal for children to be there, even if death has always dogged humankind.

Despite all the care Madelaine has given her, Rose too dies at the beginning of February. The girl finds her one morning when she arrives at her door; she is seated as if she had spent the night there, as if she had been waiting for death and wanted to be sure not to miss it. Rose, all alone. Sometimes a reason to survive is needed. Madelaine looks up whenever she passes the place where Rose's body has been hoisted, and for a moment her heart wavers with the old woman hanging there, to a slow rhythm. She places one hand on her chest, then goes on her way. She has taken the balms she knows how to use back to Ambre's place, but Rose's knowledge is gone. There is no one to take over. No one knows how. In silence Madelaine recites the ointments she prepared with Rose, and she already knows she won't be able to make them again all on her own.

The alliance of cold and hunger consume the village. First it's one, then the other. Basically, everything is connected. Madelaine continues to roam through the woods with Artaud. They don't say so but they dream of an apparition, a lost deer or even an emaciated hare they could share with their families, anything, provided it can be eaten. Hunger has reached huge proportions, they think of nothing else. They don't talk about it, to talk about it would give life to that hunger, to talk about it would arouse their bellies which, after a moment's silence, would begin thundering again, pulling at their guts. To give themselves the illusion of satiety people turn to water once again, they grow swollen with it. But after a moment, even water cannot hide the hollow in their stomach, and the sensation of suffering from an emptiness at the very core of their body explodes and drives them mad. They look for anything to eat, as if it were preferable to nibble on something rotten than die of hunger. They put little rotting carcasses on the stove to cook, and share them out, fingers trembling. They don't even ask themselves anymore how long they'd been there—no one cares, the constant state of hunger has rendered them unreasonable. As long as they can still eat. The next day the weakest among them, children and old folk, writhe in pain, and throw up the bad, germ-infested meat, and they're back to where they started, even less than that, because the bad germs have moved in, and they die, consumed from within, it's that or die plain and simple, a fine choice. The women add sawdust to the last of their bean soup to thicken it and make it go a bit further; dysentery empties their bowels and joins the bronchial diseases that the cold weather has spread all through the country; there is no way out. The children's eyes are as white as the frozen land. Entire families lie down in their freezing cottages to wait for death to embrace them, one after the other; parents watch their children die and there is nothing they can do, they themselves are as good as lifeless, their hands are empty. And this is life, dying together with no other solution, without God to save the world, even God deserted this hostile region long ago. The strongest earn the right to watch their loved ones die. The strongest steal from the weakest to live one more day.

Those who remain are hardened by hunger and effort. They are envelopes of flesh in which bones rattle together, muscles atrophy from the lack of food; they hardly realize that their strength is declining, they think it's the bad weather, their ankles twist and their arms give way, they come home and get undressed by the fire, to eat so little, to sleep, sometimes, yes, they think it would be easier if everything ended. But by the following day instinct has picked them back up. They've become animals, only the urge to live another day concerns them. Every morning Madelaine joins her cousins, wordless, devastated by the thought that they could die so easily from this hunger. They would sell their souls to have something on their plates, and their hollowed eyes tell how far they'd go to find enough to feed themselves for one more day. In the forest they scratch at the ground to unearth roots, and that is what they'll eat for supper, boiled roots that make their bellies ache, they're hungry every hour of every day, they've been hungry for years.

Madelaine sometimes sets off on her own before dawn, frantic. For Ambre. The barrenness has brought her even closer to her mother: she grabs her bony white hands and swears to her that she will not come home empty-handed. Her entire quest is straining toward her. She will fight to the blood to bring something home to feed her, even a worm, and Ambre puts her arms around her, she no longer tells her not to be afraid, the way she did at the beginning of winter, they stand holding each other, silent, frozen, starving. Léon sits slumped by the fire, where he fiddles with wood shavings forgotten in his pockets. It's out of the question now to meet others around a jug of wine, and his mood is sullen, he is weakened by the lack of food more than other folk, the alcohol had already emptied him of flesh, now his features are darkening, sagging, his fingers tremble. Ambre keeps watch to make sure he doesn't steal the little bread they have left, all trust is lost, for this reason and so many things, she sleeps in front of the dough trough.

Madelaine forces herself to get up when it's still dark. Courage has abandoned her, and strength, but for her mother . . . That's why she sits up, soundlessly, not to wake anyone, she wraps herself in her cape and pulls on her bonnet, and every dawn seizes her with the same icy breath the moment she opens the door. For a split second she hesitates. She thinks she won't be able. And then she steps forward and the day is with her, casting gray shadows over the countryside.

When Eugène's sons join her she says she couldn't sleep. The truth is that their company both comforts and disturbs her: if she finds a few frozen berries that are still edible . . . how many portions will they have to share? And what if the boys find them first? Sometimes she would like to tell them that they're on her land, and they should leave. That it's her territory and it will be her food. Of course nothing belongs to her—and anyway, more and more often she goes home with her satchel empty, or near-empty, she has to be glad of a few roots with their bland taste, she could weep. At home now it's the bread that's making her nauseous. As long as she was still picking things, Ambre added them to the dough—chestnuts, acorns, beechnuts, to make up for the shortage of flour. Now she can no longer find any. And yet it's not the pigs that are filching them, they ate the pigs long ago, too soon, they weren't big enough but the hunger was so strong. Now the barn is empty. All the barns in La Foye are empty, and the reserves, too. It was wild animals that had cleaned out the undergrowth, and when Madelaine came home two days in a row without so much as an acorn, Ambre told her it was pointless from there on. She did what the ancestors used to do, she added flour made of wood or straw to the dough, she added clay or chalk, depending on what she found, to give it volume. The bread is lumpy and horrid, and it weighs heavier than gold. They get sick. They have no choice.

In fact, thinks Madelaine, the forest is as hungry as we are. She walks through trees stricken with cold, immobile and silent. Nothing is happening here. Nothing is moving. To catch something by surprise she would have to wait for hours, and she can't—it would be the death of her. Or she would have to shake everything, to oblige nature to come out, turn everything upside down the way hunters do during their insane stalking, the horses' hooves twisting on the frozen earth, the dogs howling after their terrified prey. Madelaine could stand that even less. She goes back to the farm, walking slowly, satchel hanging; she is crushed with exhaustion and anger.

Some days there are rumors that the Ambroisies have ordered carts of flour from distant regions, that the villagers should receive them soon. This hope enables them to hold on a little longer, even when they see nothing coming. And this winter, even harder than the others, cracking their lips and hands, damaging their feet and freezing them through and through, this winter will eventually get the better of them. Madelaine looks at Eugène's sons, the layers of clothing hanging large on them, they were never so loose before. They are rapidly losing weight. To Madelaine it seems that it is getting colder and colder, but it's only because she is so thin, she has no more flesh to protect her, her freezing body eventually makes her clothing and blankets that bit colder, too. She doesn't know which way to approach the fire, facing it or with her back to it, she shivers so violently on the side turned away from the heat of the flames. She is furious, too, because she's certain that at the château they have food to eat. Not as much as before, but none of the Ambroisies will die of hunger. It turns her cheeks red, she says life is unfair, that they have taken half the wheat because they own the land. And why should the land belong to them? It's not a question the others ask themselves, it has simply always been that way. Madelaine is filled with rage. She paces through the Ambroisies' woods, and if she finds any game, nothing will stop her. When hunger takes hold, it does not know what is forbidden.

Artaud often goes with her, otherwise Ambre would not let

her stray so far into the woods. She has scoured the banks of the Basilic, but it's as if the fish, too, had frozen, the river is white and gaping. No one here likes eating the flesh of fish, with that particular taste it has, but nowadays neither Madelaine nor Eugène's sons would show such petty disgust, and if they caught any fish they'd devour them, sucking on every bone, licking the skin, mouths watering from the smell of them grilling on the fire; but the problem is, they cannot find any fish. They return to the forest. If there's an animal, even just one, they will know. Nothing will escape them. Have they eaten everything here, too, that the woods have to offer in the way of fresh meat? Madelaine inhales the icy air, and it brings no smells, she runs to examine a hoofprint, a scratching sound, some proof of passage. She searches the bushes, scans every shelter the trees might offer. She sees and hears everything, and yet nothing comes to her. The world has been emptied of all living creatures. She looks at the stones and asks Artaud, could they eat them if they ground them very fine?

At the end of February the village of La Foye looks like a jumble of motionless, frozen little clusters. Half-empty houses that are still too full, voices silenced, people crushed. Bodies are nothing more than skin pulled taut over jutting bones. More than anything there is no momentum to help a body to its feet, to go out and look for food, to carry on for another week, another day, another hour. It has been the same scene of desolation for days, the same landscape transfixed by a terrible breath of ice. In waves, the temperature stays below freezing all day long, and the vise of frost tightens around everything living. Humans, animals, plants, they can't take it anymore, what strength they have left is gathered just to keep from dying, and it's not enough. The streams and wells have frozen, Madelaine breaks the ice once a day with her hatchet to fill bowls of water, the ice is as thick as her fist. Above all, there is this silence: not a bird call, not a rustle, not a scurry. Everything escapes and hides—everything dies in its hiding place because it has not been dug deep enough, it is not warm enough, the need remains to go out for food or to lick at a frozen puddle, and the cold traps the animals on the icebound grass, a yellowed, withered grass that will never grow again, frozen to the roots. It is in this lunar world that they must survive, a world that is not made for humans.

Or for anything.

Trees split, frozen, crack open like shards of scattered wood.

Somewhere in those days they lose Léon.

He disappears when he goes out with Madelaine to look for roots. Usually, it is Ambre who goes with the girl, but Ambre is sick, she has a deep cough at night and Madelaine didn't want her mother to be out in the icy air that afternoon, it's too cold, she's afraid that exhaustion will get the better of her. And that is why Léon is with her, despite their mutual distrust, they must not go out alone, to be alone is to risk falling, and no one would ever find a trace. So Madelaine and Léon go, the two of them, enveloped in a polar fog, they no longer recognize the countryside where they were born. They left at around noon, after a clear soup that burned their throats. They plan to walk for an hour, perhaps two, to go beyond the land scoured a thousand times by others. Keep watch on the sky. Go home before dark, absolutely. They will have to turn around, whether their satchels are full or empty. Madelaine is walking ahead. Madelaine has the forest engraved in her. Madelaine pays no heed to the day turning gray and yielding to a cold dark twilight, she has come a long way, to find something to take home to Ambre. Behind her, Léon is mumbling. She doesn't listen. Léon who takes the biggest share of food because he's the man of the house, she doesn't understand why, Léon hardly works—what sort of strength could he possibly need? When the soup comes, he orders Ambre to give him more, half the pot. Madelaine and Ambre share the other half, and it's the same with the bread. So

Léon can just walk, thinks Madelaine, angry, closing her ears when he says the night is about to fall, they have waited too late to turn back, they'll be going home in the dark.

Madelaine keeps going, taking quick little steps. The cloak of fog effaces landmarks and distances. Even Madelaine hesitates. But it's that way. She turns off, searches, finds her way, looks at the blackening sky, the stars coming out, one by one. She goes faster. Léon calls out.

Madelaine. Wait.

As with those excited children who do as they please, she goes faster, drawn on by something else, the tension of a familiar path. Trees she can no longer see in the dark claw at her face, scratch her. The thought of her mother draws her on, suddenly she is overcome with worry, as if darkness were multiplying the danger of leaving Ambre alone in the house. Madelaine tries to reassure herself but she used to feel reassured for Rose as well, and yet . . . so her disquiet drives her on, she's running now, she can feel her breath scraping at her throat.

Madelaine!

It's the last time she hears Léon. She won't stop for anything, won't stop running or moving on, for her he has not existed for a long time. She's alone with the night, alone with the cold. There is no animosity in the world that envelops her, and she does not feel threatened, not really, she thinks that Léon is right, she left it late, to head home. But she knows instinctively that she is on her way back to The Rises, and a strange peacefulness comes over her. Her hands held out in front of her because of the branches, she listens to her steps on the frost, the cracking around her, she senses that animals are coming out. The cry of an owl. A rustling sound that could be anything. The awareness of time has abandoned her. Walk.

When at last she opens the door at the farm, her lips blue, her eyes open wide not wanting to close, Ambre puts her arms around her with a muffled moan. Her mother sits her down next to the fireplace, enfolds her in a blanket. She brings her a cup of hot soup, Madelaine has difficulty swallowing, her entire body is in slow motion. Gradually the pink returns to her cheeks, her skin burns, she moves her feet, shivers. The question comes only afterwards. Where's Léon? Madelaine shakes her head. She doesn't know. He was behind her.

They find him in the morning, when Eugène and Germain come to help them search the forest. Léon is sitting against a tree. At first they think he is sleeping, but his eyes are open, shadowed with a milky veil. He is only a half hour's walk from The Rises. He got lost, Eugène will say. They fetch the big horse to bring back his body, which they will clean and cloak before hanging it from the beech tree behind the barn. Ambre and Madelaine stand there gazing at the dangling parcel. There is no sadness, they are stunned. The man who was there only yesterday. Ambre says nothing, voices no reproach. She puts an arm around the girl's shoulders. She knows that Eugène will have to take care of them now and the thought is somehow troubling. But she doesn't want to be a burden. She looks at her daughter. You and I, she murmurs. We'll come through. Madelaine smiles. When they go back in, the house seems big. At night, nestled together, Madelaine wishes this would never change.

With the first signs of more clement weather, Madelaine and her cousins go to work on their frozen plots of land with the slowness of the famished. Germain has had an insane idea that only a raging hunger could have put into his skull: the shoots have frozen—except that at the end of the shoots that are only recent, there are still seeds. Open seeds, half rotten, but they are prepared to eat so much worse. If they gather all the seeds from every furrow, or even only half of them, they'll have sackfuls. The task seems huge, incongruous, dizzily exciting. Days of thaw, backs bent in cold, driving rain, they hoe, on their knees. This requires extreme attentiveness: if they dig a bit too deep, the seeds will be pushed into the earth and they'll lose them. So they set to work like ants with unremitting tiny gestures. They deposit the seeds in buckets that Madelaine regularly comes and collects. Her job is to wash the crop. Her hands purple with cold, shriveled from the water, she shakes, removes gravel and bits of grass, she rinses. When it's clean enough, she transfers the seeds to another container, and runs over to her cousins to fetch their meager pickings.

In the space of an afternoon they obtain roughly one bucket of seeds. Considering the effort all four of them have put in, it could be discouraging, but their eyes are glowing. They cannot recall how long it's been since they've seen this much food; they share it out and, this time, Madelaine demands her equal portion. Germain gives in. That morning his father told him, ordered him, You will leave some for Ambre and Madelaine.

Then it's time to go home, to heat up what remains of the seeds, for a large part it is just the husks, but not only, boil it slowly so their stomachs can take it: the houses fill with the sickly sweet smell of wheat cooking. The women oblige them to divide their rations. There will be some left over for the following day, and even the day after. It's like eating bread before it becomes bread, the main thing is to have more to eat, to give the impression that they're no longer unbearably hungry. In the comfort of the hot gruel they say they will start again the next day, weather permitting, their broken nails and scraped fingers aren't bothering them anymore, they'll go again tomorrow.

Bit by bit the frost deserts the countryside. The month of March brings a succession of days that are almost warm, with spells of cold, winter fighting back, not wanting to surrender. It's too early to sow, and they have no more seeds. The sacred bags, the ones they kept in the granary for the next year's sowing, have all been eaten, down to every last house in La Foye. They knew the risk they were taking, but famine forced their hand. They could not let themselves die of hunger when there was seed stored above their heads. They had waited as long as they could—one day at the end of January they couldn't take it anymore, they gutted the sacks. Now they must depend on the merchants, they've sent messengers. They've heard tell that in the major towns in the country, the wheat stored in the public grain houses will be released, that the seeds will arrive soon. The merchants never come in winter. They will be here this month, and the villagers have no means to pay, not all of it, they'll be debtors, next year's harvest has already been swallowed by the credit they'll be given. With each passing year they grow poorer. It would take a magnificent season. Sometimes the old folk talk about it around the fire, with blue in their eyes, those years when the wheat and the rye spilled from the granaries, they say they didn't know what to do with it all, that's not true, it's just to spice up the story. But everyone had enough to eat, enough to build up their reserves, and nowadays that time seems idyllic, no one ever thought that famine would come back so resolute, so lasting. The men of the Church say it's for the sins of the world. Everyone searches their memory for the little individual acts of unkindness that have led to this great calamity; the gang of four continue to search the earth.

The fact that in the country there are hundreds of thousands who have died of hunger does not touch them. The only thing they see is that in La Foye, out of nearly one hundred and sixty inhabitants, they have already lost fourteen. And they do not want to add to that number. They'll dig deep into the ground if they must, to where even the worms no longer go. Every day they see Eugène and his big horse go by, Eugène out looking for firewood now, since they can no longer cross the river. He gathers faggots and branches, and hitches them behind Jéricho. He calls out to his sons and Madelaine, they stop for a moment, reply with slow, sweeping gestures. It does their hearts good to see each other. To know they are all here, have refused to die, each one of them in their own way. Eugène carries wood to Ambre's farm. There is no place for emotion anymore, and yet. They look at each other, faces old before their time, emaciated, their skin diaphanous and streaked with purple veins, they hardly recognize each other. Every year counts tenfold when every day is a struggle to stay alive.

And yet.

They see each other and there's a shivering. Eugène thinks of the space that is free next to Ambre, he thinks of Léon who is dead, at a receding, but persistent distance, he says nothing, puts the wood into the barn. Ambre does not invite him to sit down, she has nothing for him, only the awareness of their physical decline that gradually kills feelings, there can be no loving a wrinkled old woman of thirty-five, whose teeth have begun to come loose. Life is an abyss, she thinks.

And yet.

He is lovely, Eugène, and so is she, in their own ways, emaciated and evaporated, a kind of beauty, indestructible, insolent, that endures despite the best efforts of fate. They smile at one another and all at once their wretchedness vanishes. They smile, nothing more, they haven't the strength, there is no future. Eugène goes away again with a small stab of warmth in his chest. Be careful, Ambre advises, the path is slippery, the rain has washed away the frost.

And for weeks a filthy swamp spreads everywhere.

It rains to overflowing, it rains and the days seem shorter again, discolored by so much grayness. In the fields Germain, Madelaine, Artaud, and Mayeul watch as the seeds run from their hands, tumble into the furrows, melt into the mire. They have to run after them, as if running after a veil borne away on the wind. Seeds so spoiled it's like eating water. But Germain will not bend. He goes back to his field and in his momentum he takes the other three with him. Clods of sticky mud, thick and heavy, feet soaked, legs that wobble and slip. No one protests. For all that the harvest will be meager, it will provide supper, or the pretense of supper, until the seeds arrive, until they are able to plant them, until those seeds produce ears of wheat. Sometimes they measure the time remaining until the next harvest, even if they mowed early, it would all be too late. To stave off the months of famine, of sickness and exhaustion, they pray for the spring to save them, but the spring means crops that won't yield before summer, and from where they stand at the moment, that means still half the year to wait, half the year to beg, half the year to die just as quickly. The merchants are their only hope, the promise of seeds and flour above all, it's now they have to eat, not a month from now, not six months. If there is no one left to do the sowing and no one left to do the reaping—Madelaine shrugs her shoulders, Well then, she says, there'll be no one left to do the eating and everything will be settled.

Somewhere in their consciousness they know how fragile they are. They don't listen, they don't look. The weak are already dead and up in the trees. The survivors belong to another race. Evening sees them stooped and exhausted; in the morning they set out again and there's a war cry deep in their chests. Can it last? They don't know, they don't ask themselves, it would be too hard. They just have to get up and head out, think of nothing else, refuse to open the door to doubt.

Resist.

Otherwise they'll fall.

Artaud cries out.

They run straight over. They pick him up, but he collapses. And suddenly Madelaine sees it. The wound. She says it. She shouts it. Germain lets go of his brother's arm, leaves him lying on the wet ground, and has a look. His leg is bleeding at the bottom, through the cloth of his breeches. What happened, he cries.

Artaud's hands are held tight against his leg, the bright red stain spreading as they watch. He doesn't answer, he's in too much pain. Besides, it's so stupid. He slipped, the hoe missed the ground. The hoe struck his leg, he felt the sharp sound against the bone, and immediately afterwards the bolt of pain. He's used to pain. Teeth clenched he says, It will pass.

They take him back to The Rises. Everyone helps, with an arm, their back, to support him. Germain has bound the wound tightly with his woolen belt, they wrapped up his leg, kneeling in the mud and the rain, now it looks like a gaiter that is too big. Artaud's face is white, like a winter dawn. He would like to send them away, to go home on his own—but he can't. Cautiously, he puts his foot on the ground. It doesn't hold, Germain catches him. The third time, it works. He leans on it, a little. This leg, abandoning him. How long will it take before he can come back to work? Aelis runs out when she sees them, still a ways off, a little cluster of figures braced to help the injured boy, that's all she can see, the mass of bodies, she knows there's something wrong.

A strange taste to the following day. For the first time Artaud is not with them. They wade through the fields and his absence burdens the land. Too often silent, Germain doesn't laugh, Mayeul doesn't chatter. At midday Germain sends the younger two home. The rain has furrowed everything, there's nothing to hope for from the empty rows, or only just. They're better off helping out at The Rises, treading through the woods in search of a bird, a field mouse, a berry. Mayeul and Madelaine leave, Germain takes a deep breath of air. He puts down his tools, sits on a rock and gazes at the horizon, over there where the mountain begins. Sometimes the desire to be alone is stronger than work or hunger or fatigue, and that is why he let the others go ahead, so he can breathe, not physically, but in his head, so he can catch his breath with those craggy mountains in the distance. He has heard tell of skies of a blueness only a sky above the clouds can possess, of air so pure it knocks your head back, of landscapes that take your breath away. The landscapes that have taken Germain's breath away up to now are fields filled with stones, because he had to turn the earth over completely in order to make it arable, and he thought he'd end up leaving his back his arms his hands with his brothers, he thought it would cost him his life, quite simply, as he gasped for air against a tree and waited for his heart to come back to him. Up there, that's not how your breath is taken from you, that much he's understood, they're talking about beauty, they're talking about something else.

Germain with his tools on the ground that he doesn't want to pick back up, is trying to grasp what that beauty might be. For him, a clog is beautiful when it's well-made, a field is beautiful because it has flourished, a tool is beautiful if its wooden handle shines with a patina and its blade cuts sharp: beauty is when things are as they should be. He senses the limits to his vision, the way in which it finds it difficult to take in the description he's been given of that mountain over there, a magical, grandiose place—and because nothing in his life has ever seemed magical or grandiose, because he suspects he could do with a little something like that, he wonders if he ought to go and see for himself, take Artaud with him, and the idea lodges in his mind.

Germain doesn't know how to name absence. He feels it in the hollow space in his guts, he turns it over and over in his head, but the words are beyond him, serve no purpose. He thinks about animals when they're weaned from their mothers—lambs, piglets, kids—how they cry for two days, sometimes three. And then it's over. They've forgotten. You can put them back in the same herd the following week, and they don't recognize each other. The bond has been broken. It's no longer mothers with their young, it's adult animals and young animals side-by-side, they each have their own life, what happened before doesn't count anymore. Germain would like to be one of those animals, so he wouldn't feel pain.

So he picks up the tools, stabs at the earth. He doesn't even try to find the seeds, it's to keep his body busy, too exhausted, so that he can command his thoughts to stop moaning, to stop being fearful and saying that injuries are dangerous. Gradually, as he yields to fatigue, Artaud's image fades further away. Am I like the animals after all, Germain wonders, am I forgetting him—already. Am I angry with him? For the injury, because he's not here, because, when you think of it, he's the one abandoning us. He's the one who's going away. But we haven't changed, we're still the same.

That evening Germain maintains his distance. Artaud is at the table with them, almost as if nothing had happened, that's what you might think, he's just a little pale maybe, a bit of sweat on his brow. Germain keeps away, it will protect him, he thinks, from emotion, he doesn't want to leave any room for emotion, that's women's business, it's work that braces him, that obsesses him, that raises him up. He looks at Artaud with his dark, guilty air. Artaud who is eating and not working. But for nothing on earth would Germain want to be in his shoes, with the pain and the shame, only it mustn't last too long, they can't take that on, he says, When will you be back?

He's seen men plow with crooked legs.

Aelis says the bone is sticking out of the flesh, that it's impossible, it has to set. If only they had a bonesetter—but Rose is dead, she was the only one who knew, who could have helped. Germain doesn't want to know. Knowing hurts. And besides, he feels strong. He does feel some remorse, but really, next to Artaud he feels solid, Artaud is white and motionless. He thinks about the men he's known who've had injuries like this, the ones who limp in the fields, or hold one arm bent back on itself. Maybe Artaud will be like them, damaged forever, something twisted that will persist, a hollow in his flesh, a force that's drained away. It doesn't concern him. It's not his fault. It's not his leg. He, Germain, is someone you can count on, he's no slacker.

Germain goes on living.

Every morning when Madelaine asks him how Artaud is doing, he replies with a shrug of his shoulders. He's all right.

But the days go by slowly, and he's not all right.

One morning Madelaine crosses the yard, goes into the house, sees Aelis pale and trembling. Artaud's leg is laid bare on the bench and what she sees is ugly—black, red, yellow. What she sees is Artaud with fever that is causing him to sweat and his hair to clump together, and then those fits of shuddering that she immediately recognizes, because she's already seen them in other people, on rare occasions, and she freezes. It's not what she thought. It's not what Germain said. In truth, the malady is something else, inside. It is there. Her eyes wide open, Madelaine goes deep inside herself, not to cry out.

She looks at Aelis and she realizes that Aelis knows. Madelaine thinks that if Rose were here, but Rose is no more. And even so: that malady—oh how hard it is to say it even in silence—that malady is not something you recover from. She remembers Rose shaking her head. You can put all the poultices you like and drink all the plants on earth, no one has ever come through it. And Madelaine doesn't want to look up at Artaud, he too has understood. The wound is hideous, the malady is deeper and more serious. If it were just his leg. But no. The malady is spreading through him, poisoning, attacking. Aelis rubs her smock between her hands. That morning, Artaud's jaw was contracting, he had incontrollable cramps. That's the sign, Aelis murmurs, and she stares at Madelaine, the terror, the unspeakable terror between them. They don't need to speak, their memory is tossing images before them. It was in the village. They've seen it, twice.

Artaud's lips are pinched as if to hold back his cries and Madelaine would like to tell him to open his mouth, because soon he will no longer be able to, but he's closed his eyes—he has gone down into his body to probe it, gone down and seen that there is nothing to be done, that he has already been taken by a force so much greater than his own, a force that is feeding on his flesh, inside he is splattered with blood, and when his body gives a start, he thinks: it's beginning.

The disease takes its time coming, as if it wanted to leave room for hope. It grants a few days, perhaps ten or more, a time when everyone thinks it will be all right, that despite the weakness they all share, Artaud will pull through with a bad leg, it's only a leg. To the fever, they respond that his body is fighting back. The fever is almost a good sign. Aelis gives Artaud a bit more food, to help.

And then the disease strikes. From then on, from the moment they all identify it, because they can no longer ignore it, they begin to look away. They no longer dare speak of it. Eugène, Germain, and Mayeul all keep their distance, focus on the hunger that gnaws at them, above all not to name that filthy scourge that is devouring the son, the brother, that disease of rust and earth that is already ravaging him. Because it is going quickly, incredibly quickly.

Madelaine was right: two days later Artaud can no longer open his mouth. Aelis is terrified by his grimace: brows frowning, lips pinched, everything is gradually seizing up, becoming rigid, suppleness is deserting him, giving him at times a sardonic mask that she refuses to look at. In the evening they all eat except for Artaud, he would like to, but his mouth won't obey him anymore. Eugène and Mayeul insert a fine metal spindle at the corner of his mouth, so they can pour in a little water, a little soup, not for long, Artaud begins to choke. Eugène has gone down to the village, even though he knows very well no one will be able to help.

The prolonged spasms in his face begin, then before long it is his entire body that is overcome. Madelaine leaves the fields, with Ambre she helps Aelis. At home all she does is keep the fire going, the rest of the time she's at the house across the way, she takes Artaud's hand when he can let her have it. The mothers see to the daily chores, but Madelaine—Artaud calls out for her, looks for her, they ask her to watch over him. In a low, terrified voice, he tells the girl about the extraordinary force that is arching his stomach and his back in movements fit to splinter his bones, that stretch his muscles to breaking point, and he cries out in agony when this happens. The first time, Madelaine runs out of the house. She comes back. He pleads. For them to put him straight again, bend him into shape, and she pulls on his arms to right him, she feels as if a huge animal is fighting with her from the other side. She doesn't have the strength. She calls to the mothers, in the end they roll Artaud around a block of wood, tying his hands to his feet to curve his backbone into a fetal position and counter the extension; it's something they once saw done in La Foye and it has stayed with them, as have the days that followed, and the growing horror. In the village one of the old folk told them not to attach Artaud anymore, that his bones and muscles would break and tear.

And so Madelaine forces herself, she promises to be there whenever he opens his eyes, there's nothing more she can do, just be there, hold his gaze, that faint, panicked glow she wishes she would never have to see again. Often she looks at the jars of ointment she brought back from Rose's, how they serve no purpose anymore, she feels like throwing them against the wall, those useless balms, if only she'd had more time to learn to offer relief, perhaps—forget about healing—simply to help. Help to die, to, but she doesn't know how, her ignorance overwhelms her.

Sometimes Aelis comes closer. Her face is inscrutable, she knows there's no hope. She is waiting for her son to die. Praying for it. So that the agony will end. She and Ambre decide to take

Artaud to Léon's place, in the farm across the way, to remove him from their terrified gazes—Eugène, Germain, Mayeul. The prospect is terrible, but life goes on, and so Artaud, the weakening son, is being put to one side, taken away, the men must keep up their strength, keep their drive; above all, their spirits must not be contaminated. Now Madelaine is alone with her mother and the dying boy. Nothing brings peace, neither the cloths she puts on his brow, nor the blankets she wraps him in, nor the smell of calming herbs.

She stays three whole days by his side. He is nothing but shuddering. His face has a blue tinge from pain and rigidity; Madelaine catches herself searching and no longer finding those fine features; beauty has fled, overpowered by suffering. She hardly recognizes him. During the attacks that contort him, make him scream, he is nothing more than animal flesh shaken with spasms, incredible strength for such a devastated body, she clings to his hands, does not leave him. She swallows her tears, Artaud is her favorite, fate is fighting her for him, and of course fate will have him, she feels the separation coming once again, and life seems terribly unjust. Maybe she had imagined something else for them; during their long spells of wandering in the forest, there had been their gazes, their sidelong smiles, that funny little burning in their guts. When their hands touched over a root, or as they handed each other the heavy canvas bag, a warmth would come. She mustn't think of it anymore, it won't happen again. Madelaine knows it, Artaud, too. During the rare moments of calm, when Madelaine tries to numb him with plants, his eyes shine on her, full of pain and yet, there is still that gentleness she misses already. She curls her fingers around his; he weeps, often. He can't take it anymore. The moments of respite serve only to heighten the fear of relapse. Madelaine is his only comfort. She is there. I will always be here, she says, overcome by this promise that will only be kept for a few days. But she believes in miracles. Insanely, absurdly, she says they will reverse fate.

On the afternoon of the fourth day, between two stifling convulsions, Artaud grabs Madelaine's arm and asks her to help. She nods, her hands are trembling with fatigue and emotion. I'll hold you, she whispers. He pushes her away. Not like that. She looks at him, her eyes grow wide, from between the jaws that will no longer open, she makes out his words: she must finish him off. If he were a creature, they would have killed him to put an end to the suffering, that's what must be done, he is not less than a creature, Madelaine, please.

But Madelaine runs away, the thought of it terrifies her. It's a very different thing from killing a pig or a hare.

Madelaine.

She presses her hands over her ears, not to hear him.

And then there is the following dawn, when Artaud's body twists backwards as if he were being torn apart by the overwhelming strength of work horses. That dawn when screams go beyond anything Madelaine has ever heard of human or animal agony. Ambre's not there, she is already helping Aelis on the other side of the yard, there is no point running over there, to do what. Madelaine leans over Artaud, his eyes have rolled upwards, the terror within. She agrees. She tells him. She waits for the fit to pass, she can do nothing before, the disease is too powerful.

Then it's morning and Madelaine is sitting alone outside on the frost-covered grass. It's one of the rare times in weeks that there has been sunshine. A pale, icy sunshine that gives no warmth, but the light is yellow and gentle, a light that changes the world, the way one looks at it, the things one does there. The frozen earth shimmers with flowers.

Perhaps the silence, too, does not weigh so heavy; so little that no one notices it, and Madelaine lies down on her back, feels the cold pierce her clothing. She closes her eyes, the cold doesn't matter. It beats at the back of her skull and she thinks she will need more than this to calm the turbulence in her mind.

She turns her wrists, places her hands flat on the ground. The tension they carry goes down into the rock, the trembling slowly leaves her—either because the ice is absorbing it, or the entire earth has begun to tremble, and for a second, Madelaine has the deep sensation that a certain order is being restored, a sad, empty order, but an order all the same.

She observes the vapor coming from her mouth, making a little cloud in the clear sky. The sun is veiled and she can look straight at it. Sometimes a bird passes in her field of vision, flies higher and higher in the golden halo of morning mist, then disappears in full flight, diving toward an unknown destination. Madelaine's heart flutters to a dull rhythm. She tries to concentrate now: to think of the others she must go and fetch, of the words she will say, first of all the blanket in which to wrap Artaud's body. Soon, she thinks. Soon she will get up and cross the yard, she will go to Eugène's farm, where they are alive, and she will announce it. They will say that it is good. That it had to end. Aelis and Ambre will weep. At the moment, Madelaine's body is charged with lead, riveted to the ground, she needs just a short moment to gather her strength, to erase the dawn and convince herself to go on. It's tugging at the corners of her eyes. With her finger she traces the streaks of tears that have wet her face, the narrow furrows they make down to her ears, down to her neck. She wishes they would never dry, so she'll remember.

She senses Artaud's motionless body beside her. She doesn't look at it, doesn't touch it. She simply knows he's there. At last Artaud is at peace, that's the way it must be, she mustn't weep.

Madelaine wipes her hatchet and her knife to erase the blood. She wishes she could erase the images, too, when at dawn they left the place of shelter, Artaud shaking with spasms, he wanted to see the sky, and they came soundlessly away, Madelaine's eyes were red, but he was the one who said it first—You mustn't cry. He lay down exactly as she is lying now, with the spasms bringing the shuddering more and more often, his breath coming in fits and starts. He looked at the clouds for a moment, the outline of the trees slowly taking shape in the dim still-gray light of day; then he closed his eyes and she knew it was time. Like with the animals. First a blow with the flat of the hatchet blade to stun him, then the knife to his jugular.

A few seconds.

Artaud didn't move, didn't struggle. Madelaine knows the gestures, she was sure of her act, only it wasn't an animal lying there before her, she mustn't hesitate, mustn't falter.

Since it was all futile.

Artaud felt nothing.

Madelaine looked at the blood on the knife-blade, on her hands, her arms. That blood was another matter. She vomited bile on the grass, a yellow stain amid the frost, it came all of a sudden.

When at last she gets up, her head is spinning. She spreads her arms, feels as if she is floating, she's not very well. She breathes in. Once, twice. So deep that her heart could fail. Then she walks along the house and across the yard, her hands on the little wall. There is a faint light at Eugène's farm. Suddenly she is eager to smell the morning porridge, the bad bread, eager to go to her mother, to rush into her arms, in silence.

It is Aelis who sees her first. They are all there in the room that is barely warm. They turn around. They know. Is it done? asks Aelis in a low voice, and Madelaine nods, she doesn't say what is done, or that it's too heavy for her. She wonders if there are words to tell of Artaud's last dawn, she would like to forget, she knows it's impossible, that all her life it will be impossible, she's the one who was left with him. Her gaze searches for Ambre, but it is Aelis who comes to her, her face inscrutable, Aelis who opens her arms, then closes them around her. Ambre comes and joins them. They hold each other tight, the men watch from a distance, don't dare. The women cling to one another to keep from falling. The sorrow for the dead boy holds them together.

Spring comes all at once, fragile, the fields call to the seeds. There is urgency, exhorting exhausted bodies to put in a new effort, offering nothing in exchange: they must plow, plant, cover over. Once again, necessity sweeps sorrow away, hunger crushes thought. Madelaine walks behind Germain, shoulder to shoulder with Mayeul, Eugène has gone back to hauling. No one speaks about Artaud. It has been a month. A month is a long time. Sorrow lurks deep inside, does not show its face. Sorrow fades quickly, there is too much to do, to survive.

The convoy of grain finally arrived in the Hinterland. The villagers paid a fortune for the wheat, rye, and buckwheat, for the illusion of salvation, anger, too, the price had risen yet again. The merchants came with a guard to protect themselves from the shouts of the poor. In some towns, excited crowds pillaged the carts and injured the tradesmen; if the beggars don't want to cough up, they'll get nothing. Ambroisie-Father sent for a second convoy for the distribution to his peasants; this time it was the master who paid, they've been talking about it among themselves, the most embittered say that it's to spare his laborers, but most of them, in private, are thankful. They've been eager to get back to work, as soon as the land was ready, that's all they've been waiting for. They want to prove to Ambroisie-Father that they are grateful. The yoke no longer weighs upon them, they consent, old Magne has gone back to heating the oven, the bread leaves its heady smell inside the cottages. Of course the master will take a greater share of the harvest this year: he has to build up his granaries again. They agree to this, too. To them, servitude seems normal, with each passing day their lives are at stake, they don't think six months ahead, the future is a notion they avoid. We'll see, they say.

And so April marks the beginning of the sowing. Germain works like an ogre, huge and powerful, he never goes home with Madelaine and Mayeul at the end of the day. He stays in his fields until the night is pitch, until his eyes cannot take it anymore, or his back, or his arms, he doesn't want it said that Artaud is missing, he works for both of them. Sometimes he lights a brazier so he can go on longer. Mayeul comes back with a chunk of bread, helps him for one last hour. In the darkness that takes them back to The Rises, he holds his older brother's hand, and Germain closes his eyes with exhaustion.

Ambre and Madelaine have moved into Eugène's place. The twins had spoken about it after Léon died, now the space left by Artaud is enough to convince them: they'd do better to assume responsibility for a single dwelling. Someday the other farm will be occupied again, when Germain takes a wife, and Madelaine will have Rose's little house, and they picture The Rises coming back to life, flourishing, expanding; to oppose absence and death they must fill the space, must try to hope. Eugène and his family sleep in one big bed on the left-hand side of the room, Ambre and Madelaine settle in next to them, before the table, before the kitchen and the hearth.

The sisters confront the disaster, the two of them. Of course it's not what they'd hoped for, neither Artaud's death, nor Léon's, although Léon . . . but, no, they cannot say that, they didn't want this, it's just that now that it's behind them: they are making the best of their misfortune. Sometimes they look at each other and think that the distance between the two farms has been done away with at last, but at such a price. Léon's death brought the two sisters together and Aelis sometimes sighs when she thinks of her brother-in-law, she owes this to him, and then she corrects herself, fate robbed her of two sons, there's nothing to be happy about. And yet Aelis feels lighthearted. She bites her lip, she mustn't, but a restrained joy has returned, Ambre's presence fills her with delight, something has been reborn in her. Once again the two women find their childhood closeness, the pleasure of doing every chore together, it's no longer so hard, together, why didn't we do this sooner, Aelis wonders. She doesn't notice that Eugène is lost in similar thoughts, his gaze fixed upon Ambre, it doesn't interest her, it doesn't exist.

The spring is deceptive, mild, almost warm, come too soon after their sorrows. At the end of the day Germain sits at the edge of a patch of land with Madelaine and Mayeul. Their brows are damp with sweat, they feel good, and then memory interferes and happiness fades, happiness that is never total and never lasts for long. They wonder what will come when they've planted their warm fields, what bad things will seek to counterbalance the world, since something beautiful always comes with something ugly, and it starts again, they cannot help but be fearful, even Madelaine who is fearless, who will return blow for blow with fate, but what will be will be. They are wary of springtime. It puts on airs, spins around, gets carried away, gives no warnings. One day everything will collapse. A day of frost, a day of war, a day of death. Life cannot be trusted. From generation to generation the elders have passed on the memory of the plague that killed one man in three, all it took was one ship full of infected rats, it began in summer, in July, only a month earlier no one knew of this pestilence, no one could have foreseen what was about to happen. Their entire existence rests on such uncertainties. There is no infallible future.

Madelaine scrutinizes the mildness of the air, the direction of the wind, the color of the clouds in the sky. If she could, she would sit on their fields the way a hen sits on her eggs, her arms spread to protect them, she would gather them under her, she would cover the young shoots to keep them from frost. They just have to hope. They have to trust—it's difficult, when they distrust everything, they believe only in their hands and sometimes hands can do nothing. At times, when the fear comes over them, they rush to church, the same church that has damned them, because all of this—hunger, cold, ruined harvests—all this misfortune, in the end, it's because of them, humankind, they reap what they sow. And Madelaine cries out in silence that it's not true, she knows it so very well, there is no link between what they plant and what they receive, they have put all their hearts into it, and their hearts have been broken. Madelaine says she won't go back to church, Ambre forces her, in these times she won't have others pointing at them. And besides, that's not where the next misfortune will come from; but for now, no one knows.

Ordinary life resumes in the Hinterland. Eugène and his horse go down to the ferry at dawn, the two remaining sons and Madelaine take the road for the fields. The wheat has begun to rise. Wherever you look, the tender green shoots cover the planted ground, standing out clearly against the plots left fallow, where a black and yellow vegetation emerges from winter. Germain has taken over a new plot, six hundred square yards of dead ferns and thorns, in the beginning he said it would be for next year, but his impatience betrays him, he sets to work, and Madelaine and Mayeul do likewise. They clear, cut, turn over the soil. It's also the opportunity to try the implement one of the villagers has lent them, a tool that will allow them to save on days of work by slicing through the soil to break it up, and Germain says he'll order one if it turns out to be worth it. For the moment, they don't know, they use it clumsily, they are learning. Germain slowly grows accustomed to the plowshare, puzzled because the ard requires two workers, one to pull it the way an ox would pull it if they had one, and the other to steer with the handle, pressing the tool into the ground. The work is exhausting for the one who is pulling, and Germain is the only one capable of pulling with sufficient strength to move the ard forward. The resistance of the soil continually causes the implement to jolt as he progresses along the rows, lacerating his shoulders, which bear the marks of burned skin. The work goes more quickly than with a spade and hoe, although it is harder; however, the tool has been lent to them and this is their only chance to make the land cultivable before the season, so he is determined, he uses it as much as he can, not to have regrets, and his regret is the absence of an ox. Eugène's big horse would do an even better job, but that's something that Germain doesn't have either, Jéricho hauls wood and his father needs him, he won't ask. It would be stupid to think of forfeiting one job for the sake of another, and so there is only Germain to take the place of the ox, to breathe heavily in the spring sun. He won't last all day, now and again he picks up the spade or the hoe, he gives some thought and concludes, what on earth: doing this, to get some rest. When he hitches himself to the ard again, Mayeul and Madelaine steer it behind him, steering requires only a normal degree of strength. Madelaine did try, however: one time, when Germain, exhausted, beside himself, had tossed the tool to the ground, she looked up and said, I can do it, too. Germain let her try. Straining with all her might, leaning forward to a degree where she was almost parallel with the ground, Madelaine managed to drag the plow forward. For a few seconds, Germain believed she'd do it. He thought they'd be able to share the work, to take turns, that it would be all right. Incredulous, but relieved. And then the girl hesitated. She persevered, calling to her guts for a cry of rage that would help her pull further, calling to Mayeul, fully aware that he couldn't let go of the handle, and she was the one who yielded, removed the harness, tears in her eyes. She picked up some pebbles and tossed them at the implement, she stamped on it, and Germain ran over to stop her, Madelaine don't do that. I wanted to help, she spat, her voice trembling with anger and spite. It doesn't matter, said Germain. I'll manage. Next year we'll ask to borrow Magne's ox, we'll figure it out, it will be easier, this tool isn't meant for men. Germain put on the harness, took a deep breath, silenced his aching muscles. As for Madelaine, she made an even greater effort, stabbing with the hoe. She wants to be strong, as strong as Germain.

There's no reason. She will show them all, and her arms become ropy, the bones on her back are prominent, a body that has no fear of fatigue. Her legs carry her beyond what is possible because everything is possible, she thinks, if she carries on, they will finish in time. So they will plant late vegetables—cabbage that can be picked all winter, and peas, to fill their bowls and their stomachs, it's the first time that they've planted this many, up to now Germain tried on a small patch of land, that's all. The thaw has galvanizes them, they are making the most of the fact that the ground is no longer soaked, the hoes don't get stuck, the clay is less resistant. Once again they enjoy the tired pleasure of taking a break in the shade of a tall tree when the Angelus has rung at midday. They eat their brown bread, they call it dogs' bread, from the time when, during the great hunt, they had to feed the masters' dogs with bran.

At the farm, Ambre and Aelis steal time from the day to chat in the sun, mending a piece of clothing or preparing the soup. In this they are original, the women here work in shadow, inside the house, they only go out to draw water from the well or to feed the animals, outdoors is for men. But Ambre and Aelis open up under the blue sky, their skin offered to the gentle warmth of the air. They sit on large square stones that serves as a bench, or on the little wall, or on the old oak plank, they throw their heads back and laugh, then return to their work. They talk about their children, sometimes hesitantly, about their men, now only one man, about the empty house they will have to air out to get rid of the humidity. Aelis sends the hired boy to weed the vegetable garden on the other side of the buildings, she doesn't want to be disturbed, she leads Ambre to the end of the yard, then to the other side of the path, to pick plants; they talk slowly, cheerfully, peacefully, savoring every word let loose in the sunlight, mocking the mean things the village gossips would say if they could see them—straying so far out of doors, the gossips who would say that they don't work hard enough, that working in the sun is not working, what are they thinking. They would say it's not reasonable, and indeed it's not reasonable. Not because of the sun—they're wrong about that—but rather because of the sound they hear suddenly that day.

A sound they recognize at once and which compels them to their feet, their faces very pale. Because they've made a mistake, they've strayed a bit too far from the houses, they realize right away. They look toward the farms, in vain, they are in the wrong place, neither to one side or the other, vulnerable out on this deserted path where they are so visible, too visible, and Aelis thinks of a mouse emerging in the middle of a field, how the dogs catch it because there's no hiding place anymore, she thinks how they shouldn't have, and it's too late: she takes her sister's hand and they turn away as if that could make them invisible, the sound is already on the path, pounding against the pebbles. The sound of the gray horse that belongs to Ambroisie-Son, now turning his horse in slowing semi-circles; he sees them, and stops suddenly, yanking hard on the reins.

And Madelaine, that same day at the same time, Madelaine is coming up the path to the farms, walking quickly. In the field, the ard struck a rock hidden underground. Germain came to an abrupt halt, they tried to disengage the implement, all of them together, but it was stuck fast, there was nothing to be done. Germain has sent Madelaine to get an iron bar to dislodge it—a bar, and a sledgehammer, she has taken the wheelbarrow to transport them more easily. She's hurrying because she's eager to smash the rock, eager for them to bang it and lever it and bang again, it will smell of burned stone, she loves that smell of sparks floating in the air, Madelaine is headed toward The Rises, to where Aelis and Ambre are, and now, Ambroisie-Son.

Madelaine is still out of sight of the houses when she hears the sound, and freezes.

Beyond a doubt, the sound is coming from the farms, she has difficulty identifying it, it's not a usual sound.

And it's not the galloping of Ambroisie-Son's gray horse that petrifies Madelaine, because the horse stopped a good while ago. It's another sound. Shouts, perhaps.

Not shouts.

Screams.

Women, Madelaine realizes.

So she drops the wheelbarrow to one side and runs. She doesn't know what is happening. She doesn't know what awaits her beyond the last hill, nor what she will find in her mother's house or in Aelis's house, and the terrible wailing is coming from there. For a moment she thinks the pig is having its throat cut—but there's no more pig to kill, they ate it long ago, and Madelaine remembers, she was the one who bled it, but it would make her feel better to imagine that the sound is coming from an animal because deep inside she has understood that what she's hearing, up there, is human. Or not quite human anymore, a sound of such despair or terror that the screams go searching for help in distorted, animal sounds.

And as she runs Madelaine begins calling in a shrill voice that echoes what is before her. A colossal fear is dragged out of her body, new, terrifying, fear and at the same time unspeakable rage, because Ambre or Aelis is being assaulted, she's sure of it, Madelaine cannot breathe, cannot go fast enough, feels the tears running to the corners of her eyes, wait for me, she thinks, wait.

Her eyes devouring the last hill.

But behind it—this, the girl doesn't think about, she just wants to get there and find out, children don't understand that sometimes it would be better not to know.

Behind it: suddenly she's there.

Within eyeshot.

What she sees first, because it's biggest, is Ambroisie-Son's gray horse. And the horse is jittery, terrified, no one is holding him. No one is riding him. The rest is on the ground.

The rest—the man and the two women, and further away the dogs howling, pulling at their chains. The man on top of the first woman, whose skirt has been pushed up to her waist, and the other woman on her knees just next to them, as if stunned, and Madelaine is too far away but she shouts anyway, shouts because of the gleam of the blade in Ambroisie-Son's hand, caught glinting in the sunlight of a too-warm month of May, the long blade, the metal, and then the blood and suddenly everything is red. Beneath the Son, the woman is not moving.

Madelaine covers the last few feet roaring like a wild animal. The Son sees her, begins to get up, his dagger in his hand; a huge smile crosses his face when he sees the child running toward him, such an imbecilic child, running she too, like the other woman who wanted to stop him and whom he thrashed. And with a thrust of his hips he rises to his feet, amid the dress and the inert body beneath him; he adjusts his trousers, he waits. He can see the hatchet at Madelaine's side as she reaches for her belt, and now he laughs, watching as she runs toward him, pulling out her weapon and he shouts, Come on, then! He laughs, spreading his arms, because he's the master and nothing can touch him. He pictures his own dagger streaming with the dead woman's blood—she struggled, that one, she hit him with a stone she'd hastily picked up, he can feel his forehead is still bleeding a little, and then the anger, she deserved everything she got, Ambroisie-Son on top of her and the knife in her heart, afterwards, to punish her—he pictures that same blade entering the child's belly with an almost disappointing ease, or cutting her throat, and that's what's making him laugh, yes, laugh.

And there's that sound again—suddenly, the sound is terrible.

It's the echo, on impact, of bones shattering, the cracking of a body caught in a full flight, caught completely unawares, and a cry, a roar—Madelaine had thrown her arms behind her to gather momentum and as with the deer, as with the dead trees she's been practicing on for years, with a scream she has hurled the hatchet at Ambroisie-Son. She put all her rage into her scream: for the lost woman at the Son's feet, for the hunger, for the poverty, for her dog, for Artaud—years of latent hatred and tamed fury. But Madelaine has not been tamed, and the Son senses something different, that he doesn't understand, that doesn't touch him—he would never have believed a child was capable of throwing a weapon this far: he thought she was going to come to fight hand to hand, with her ridiculous urchin's strength, he was waiting for her, his blade held high, she'd have no skill in handling a hatchet—such a pathetic attempt. And then he understood, with absolute clarity: the weapon had left the child's hand and was flying through the space between them at a speed that left him no time at all. A few fractions of a second during which, incredulous, he saw out of the corner of his eye his gray horse flee in a panic—the horse galloping toward the forest, and he thought, it will take hours to catch it, how annoying, and at that very moment, the hatchet blade entered his breastbone—and that is where it's coming from, this sound of bones shattering.

The Son falls to his knees. Fingers tight around the metal, in such pain: he looks at the girl who comes to a halt without ever having slowed her pace, and he thinks he is alive, since he is looking at her, he thinks he is going to get up again and stab her with his dagger, cut her throat, eviscerate her, slice her to pieces, this little trollop who has dared to strike him, dared to hurt him, fury gets the upper hand, he opens his mouth to shout, and the blood pours onto his shirt, and he is paralyzed with shock. A moment later, Madelaine is on him. She pulls out the hatchet and Ambroisie-Son moans in pain; he waves the dagger in front of him, but the child has already stepped back to avoid it, before she rushes forward again, and then he will think that from the start he has been overconfident, he didn't gauge how quick the girl is, nor how strong, he thought it was impossible, and the thought comes to an abrupt halt in a searing flash of pain and, in a daze he sees his knife on the ground.

The blood-stained knife has fallen into the folds of the dead woman's dress, and his own hand—half-severed by a second blow of the hatchet—is now hanging useless at the end of his arm. And Ambroisie-Son understands that he's in great danger, here too he understands too late, as Madelaine brings the hatchet down a third time, this time she opens his belly and all his innards all his guts and viscera, and the man before her collapses once and for all.

Four

And that is what Eugène comes upon, once he has hurried home with the big horse, alone now that the boy sent to fetch him has run off the other way, as Aelis had told him to do—or was it Ambre?—and from up there, not a sound can be heard, not a cry, everything is utterly still. A quilt has been laid over a body, but the rest is exactly the same as it was when the surviving woman put her hands over the boy's eyes so he would not see and ordered him to go find Eugène, to go without looking back and without stopping, and the boy did as he was told. And after that, as the woman had also instructed him, he cut through the fields to round up Germain and Mayeul, not knowing why—and then he went home with his chunk of bread in his pocket, a little afraid, it all happened so quickly, he's not used to such things, he doesn't like it.

That is what Eugène's pounding heart takes in as his gaze is passing the last hill, just as Madelaine did, two hours earlier, in all its brutality: the quilt, the body of a dead woman, two figures sitting arms by their sides, amid the chaos, dazed.

This thing that signals the end of a life, the life from before, because Eugène was right, nothing will ever be the same, and now he is running heavily, tugging the big golden horse behind him as it makes the ground tremble. He doesn't know which sister has survived, both are splattered with blood, he cannot tell whether it's Ambre or Aelis, this woman who is wringing her hands and weeping, he would like to ask her, he would like someone to tell him, there, right away, but he has a premonition, the worst is there under the quilt. And fear tears at his chest and seizes upon his gaze, he has already understood, and suddenly Madelaine is clinging to him and crying, It was me.

It was me who.

Eugène looks at her, his mind wavering. He knew it. He has always sensed that this girl would bring misfortune, he thought the feeling would go away, or that misfortune would come later, in some other form, elsewhere. He could not resent her for something that did not exist. But now it has come. And so he pushes Madelaine to one side, his eyes wide, staring at the thick canvas which he slowly lifts up. He is sure of what he will find underneath, the chaos around him leaves no doubt. And yet against all reason he hopes. Have pity, let it not be *him*; and to identify Ambroisie-Son at that moment, dead, is a blow to the heart, as if his prayer could have erased reality, as if for an instant he had believed in the possibility of a miracle. More than anything, he would have liked not to recognize the dead man lying there at his feet, let it be anyone else and he would have dealt with it, but not the Son, not that man. Eugène turns to the surviving woman, who is clinging to him, sobbing; he refuses to listen to the words he already knows, they are lost, they will all be hanged, they will be tortured, one by one they will be cut into long strips of flesh as a lesson, never to lay a hand on the masters, and this too he knows, he would never have—it was she, the girl, she told him as much, she shouted as much. Eugène takes his face in his hands.

How to think when his heart is in a panic. How to organize insane, useless thoughts, because he can throw himself at Ambroisie-Father's feet, he can offer his life, they will kill them all, as an example, for the sake of the masters' justice, to avenge their blood. No one will get out of it, not even Mayeul, the youngest, there is no mercy for families who lay a hand on the masters.

Die, all of them.

The villagers will be prohibited from giving them a decent

burial, and their remains will be left to the animals that feed on carrion, birds or mammals, their corpses will fill the air of La Foye with their stench, all the way to the Basilic, and their souls will wander forever along its banks. Damned in this world and in the next—and so.

And so he has to think quickly and clearly, he has to decide if they will let themselves be killed or if they will attempt something mad that, to the best of Eugène's knowledge, no one has ever dared before, but it's his blood that is poised on the edge of the abyss, his sons his flesh, and even little Madelaine who has brought them to the threshold of hell; suddenly he makes his choice: they must try to live. He reaches for the surviving woman's arm, looks deep and hard into her eyes. He would like to ask her who she is, but the gaze facing him, that gaze replying in silence and then something else, too, later he will remember that everything began to shift the moment he saw what this gaze was telling him, ordering him to do, from that moment on, when he nods, catching himself just in time, and he murmurs her name in a leaden voice:

Aelis?

And in a tremor the woman lifts her face of tears and blood.

Abruptly Eugène pulls the quilt to one side, and sees the mutilated body, all of it; he must look away. Focus on the quilt: he rolls Ambroisie-Son's corpse onto it, sends Madelaine to fetch a rope, then he fastens it tight around both ends of the quilt. Trussed up like this, the Son inspires no more fear than the flies that are already converging upon the smell, and Eugène pushes him to the edge of the yard, and for all that he is terrified, it's not by the remains, it's by what he is doing. He stands motionless for a few seconds when the time comes to lift Ambre in his arms and carry her into Léon's house, and Madelaine see the tears on his face, tears tracing a line through dust and blood then falling to the ground, she says nothing. She looks at Eugène then she looks at Aelis and that's all.

You have to leave.

While the girl's eyes open wide, she doesn't flinch. She knew before Eugène even said it that flight was her only chance of salvation. Her reaction leaves her on edge, animal, unburdened by questions, she is not in a state to reason—otherwise, why would she run away, when no one saw her, but maybe that boy, all the same, maybe a villager saw her running, from afar, all it takes is one doubt, when Ambroisie's troops start coming, and everyone will dissolve with fear and tongues will say things they don't know just to send the soldiers elsewhere. Aelis has put a hand in front of her mouth to stifle her sobs, and in the house she takes a cape and puts it on Madelaine's shoulders, gives her a bundle which she has packed with a large loaf of bread and some lard and a few coins she had put aside. But she shakes her head, shakes Eugène's arm, he lowers his eyes—the child cannot go alone, and Eugène tells her to go and get Jéricho, the horse is grazing a bit further away. Then he takes hold of Madelaine's shoulder without looking at her.

You're going to take the horse and I'll tie Ambroisie-Son onto his back. You'll walk for three nights along the Basilic without crossing it, so The Crone won't see you. You will stop only during the day, and then you'll hide—and when you find a place where you can conceal this body forever, bury it, cover it with earth and stones so that nothing and no one can ever remove it from the grave where you have put it, that is what you will do. Then you'll continue on your way. You won't come back here, not until it's forgotten, not until ten years have gone by. You'll keep walking straight ahead until you reach another country, and we won't know you anymore. That's the price you will pay to survive. I'm giving you Jéricho. Now get ready.

Madelaine, in tears, turns around, there are shouts from behind her, more shouts she thinks, she would like to press her hands over her ears, never to hear again, either the shouts or Eugène's words. Germain and Mayeul are there. They are out of breath, their shouts are like moans, panting, they look at the path and the strange bundle rolled up on the ground. They see the traces of the struggle, long fissures dug into the ground, and the blood that has left brown spots on the grass, and everything crushed before them, and briefly they recoil. With a gesture Eugène summons them to be silent, and tells them. A few hard, cruel phrases, eyes narrowed, fists clenched. They look up at Aelis.

They don't move.

Nobody moves, not even time.

To take in the improbable reality.

Only their breath forming waves in the air.

Then Eugène breaks the silence and starts up the world again, Eugène who tells Germain: Help me. They take the quilt at either end and hoist it onto the horse's back, bind it so tightly that it will take a knife to undo their knots, as if they were afraid that Ambroisie-Son could untie himself and stand there, as if it were the devil himself they were binding so tightly.

Eugène sends Aelis to wash her sister and dress her to hide her wounds. They will say that she had an accident, they will have to prepare their lie, they don't have much time, And you—Eugène points a finger at his sons: No one saw anything. Ambre died and that's it. And Madelaine—Madelaine has gone to start an apprenticeship in another town, she's been placed with a master craftsman, they'll remember this, won't they, they nod, dazed.

Finally he turns to Madelaine and murmurs, Go. Go right now. We don't know when they'll start worrying about the little master and you have to be long gone well before that.

Go?

Mayeul cries out.

Go where?

Madelaine forces a smile to reassure him, boasting that she's going to the ends of the earth. Inside, everything is fracturing, it's like what she knows from years ago, before she came here, everything vanishing, she is already alone.

What about me? asks the youngest boy.

No not you.

I'm going to the ends of the earth, too, says Mayeul, and Eugène raises his hand and roars, and everything falls silent around them.

She doesn't look back. She said farewell, there were brief embraces, except for Aelis, who held her tight and long in her arms, in tears. And Madelaine looked her straight in the eye. She didn't say anything, she didn't need to. Aelis knows. That Madelaine cannot be fooled. Germain and Mayeul will realize someday, perhaps, men aren't that observant, are less attentive. As long as the house is kept and there's soup in the bowl.

But Madelaine.

She smiled. She won't tell. She wishes Aelis had confided in her, even though she understands it's impossible, the others mustn't know. It's a secret she'll take with her. A tiny little secret, compared to the tornado that has ravaged their lives, she will keep it deep within, buried, invisible, derisory.

It wasn't Ambre who died, it was Aelis. Eugène and Ambre sealed their silent pact with the still-warm corpses at their feet—Ambre has taken her sister's place, nothing will be said. There is the guilty thought that things should have been like this from the start, the vague notion of a reparation, of redress, of consolation.

Ambre leans against Eugène and watches her go, her Madelaine, her daughter, and Madelaine recalls the few words they exchanged just before. Her only hope: Eugène told her not to come back, not until ten years had passed, in ten years she will be there. In moments of chaos, all it takes is a tiny light to cling to and survive. It will pass quickly, thinks Madelaine, but she knows that no, the days will seem endless, the hardship of life has caught up with her yet again. She doesn't want to think about what is waiting for her. She's not afraid. But she's angry.

Eugène has told her to go, he said it was late, that with Germain and Mayeul they had to clean up, to rake the ground, erase all trace of the struggle, to tear up the tufts of grass that are red with blood and bury them beneath the manure pile. Eugène wanted to see her gone, the separation is wrenching. He murmured that once she was out of sight it wouldn't be the same, the wound would be less sharp, he would speak in the past tense.

So Madelaine doesn't look back, this is it. She is leading the big horse by his tether, and she is on her way. From the sound of furtive movement behind her, she can tell that Eugène would not wait until she'd gone beyond the end of the path. Germain and Mayeul have accompanied her as far as the little wall, heads bowed, not daring to look at her. The sons who will stay behind. The sons who are bound by fate, who cannot leave, cannot desert. The very fate which, before his sons, had bound Eugène to The Rises, when he had thought, until life decided otherwise, that he'd be roaming the world—this fate means you can get over anything, submit to anything, and the boys know it, they were the first to falter, duty is written in their blood. Eugène saw the fugitive gleam of doubt in their gazes, the way they looked at Madelaine and then the farm, and he understood the terrible dilemma, but not for a moment did he give them any choice: with one hand on the eldest boy's arm he ordered them to prepare the tools. He had come between Madelaine and his two sons, who were looking at him defiantly; he'd broken the bond between his boys and the girl. However, deep down they had already relented, it was just that they needed time to accept, time to digest, for it to stop causing these burning knots in their throats and in their guts, it would have to be all right, with those terrible words that have clung to them from birth and will cling to them until their the last day: that's just the way it is.

And thoughts went through their heads, Germain and Mayeul saw their father without his horse, now only the land would enable them to live, land that Eugène could not cultivate on his own, of course they had to stay. From now on there would be Madelaine on one side, and on the other: themselves.

It was not Eugène's arms holding them back, keeping them from following her. They themselves agreed not to. And there is sorrow in the sons' clenched jaws, a tight knot they can neither swallow nor dislodge, it is emerging from nose and eyes, but there is not a word, not a sound, and Eugène pretends not to see.

Madelaine and the horse have vanished behind the hill.

The sons get busy, it occupies their minds; they only straighten their backs once the earth has been completely swept and rid of anything that might have happened there earlier that afternoon. They dig a hole a bit further away to bury Aelis's and Madelaine's soiled clothing, they pour out barrowfuls of wood to cover the disturbed earth—wood that had been neatly stacked under the lean-to and which they have brought out and tossed here and there, as if they had just collected it in the forest and left it there to dry.

In the house Ambre washes her sister's body where it lies on a mattress. She dresses her in clean clothes, the ones she kept for special occasions, to wear to baptisms and weddings and funerals; Aelis's last garment, which will go with her for eternity, what will remain of it once she's buried and the months and years have covered it over. Ambre weeps, soundlessly, something has come apart inside her. The grief is drowning her, she knows it will, for a time, then it will depart, even for the two of them, even for twins, a scar a little deeper and then, there it is, life knows no interludes, they have to think about what comes next. Think about the extreme-unction that Aelis has not received, and the testament she did not have time to dictate, which will prevent her from being buried in the graveyard; they have to send for the priest, talk with him and perhaps come to an arrangement, they have to rehearse the lies they will tell, with Eugène—the accident, the absence of Madelaine and the workhorse, how it can all hold together. It's too much, thinks Ambre, getting used to being called by her sister's name for a start, the fact that Germain and Mayeul will say *mother* to her, and if she turns around to looks for Aelis? I'm Aelis—she tries to hammer it into her head, then she closes her eyes, frowns to make it stick, tears stream down her face, she stands still.

And if they say nothing.

Bury Aelis at the end of the garden. Make her a grave with stones, a grave that Ambre will cover with flowers to beg forgiveness, but nothing will forgive the damnation of her sister's errant soul; that is perhaps even more terrifying than the specter of them being put to death by Ambroisie's soldiers, because afterwards, Heaven would terrorize them all, men women children. The soul comes before the living. It's unthinkable to—unthinkable, and yet, if they hide the fact Aelis is dead, Ambre rather, there will be no connection possible with the disappearance of Ambroisie-Son, with the gray horse who returned to the stable on his own, no one will be able to establish a link, no one will follow their covered tracks.

But they don't have the courage, or the imagination. They are forcing themselves. It might be simpler, almost more restful, to confess and die right away. No no, Ambre takes hold of herself, she must protect the children: only their silence—they, the parents, only the quality of their deception will save Madelaine and the boys. She lowers her head and says again, murmuring. The important thing is not to die.

Not to speak.

Madelaine sent to learn another trade. The villagers will say that, with Léon's death, this was foretold, there was not enough money in the little farm and Eugène cannot feed everyone, they will say it was for the best, to entrust Madelaine to others, they would have done the same, the country is too poor. And Aelis, she'll have to remember to say Ambre, Ambre stumbled in the yard, had a bad fall, died instantly, or almost, a few hours, she hit her skull, that has happened in the village, too, everyone knows it can happen.

In fact, Ambroisie-Son should not be dead.

Ambre-now-Aelis is thinking as fast as she can. Yes, that might work. The problem is Ambroisie-Son's gray horse. The horse will eventually make its way back to the château and people will know there's something wrong. Whereas if neither the horse nor the Son ever returns—then anything is possible. The Son is mad. He could have left the country, on a whim, abducted a beautiful woman, all sorts of stories will be told, all sorts of things imagined. There's nothing violent about an absence; a disappearance isn't a death. They will look for him, obviously, but they'll find nothing, and Ambroisie-Father will curse his boy who scorns all rules and conventions, will curse the empty chair to his right at the grand table where they have their meals. The Son has sisters who are already married, with children who will come into the inheritance, gradually they will replace him, they will skip a generation, that's also something you sometimes see, even often.

But there's the horse.

Ambre closes the door to the house and goes out into the yard to call Eugène.

They each take a basket with a few berries, still green, in case they meet any other wanderers. In their clothing they've concealed long thin knives, like those used to slaughter the pigs. They left as soon as they'd finished burying, sweeping, hiding, until nothing in the vicinity of The Rises could be seen. They cut through the woods to get as close as possible to the château without being seen; after that they scatter, returning slowly in the direction of the farms, to the place where the horse first bolted; they form a screen between the horse and the stable, stalking their prey, hoping against hope that they will cross paths.

Four of them, crisscrossing the forest. They're crazy to think they will find the Son's mount, but Ambre said fate owes them something, misfortune has struck too hard. So they nodded and set off, hearts pounding, holding their breath as they part ways, Eugène to the far left, then the boys, then Ambre herself. A line moving slowly, methodically forward, as night begins to fall, the same night that is masking the horse and may already have compelled the soldiers to worry about their master. More than anything, they dread returning to The Rises without having caught the horse, they tremble at the thought of seeing their four figures at the end of the night, arms at their sides, empty-handed, and then dawn will come to bring new fears, dawn and the threat of the horse going home without the Son and the men let loose on their tracks like a pack of dogs. For the moment, they sweat with terror in the soundless night, their ears on the alert, they are crushed with silence. Sometimes a little rodent scurries past their legs and they give a start, wipe the sweat from their brows. The moon struggles to shine through the foliage of the tall trees, half hiding them but making it hard to see as well, they open their eyes wide to know where they are, they make out the shape of a steed where there is no steed, they rub their faces.

Eugène, who has gone the farthest, constantly brings his attention back to the undergrowth. The images of that afternoon are haunting his memory and make him lose his concentration; it is as if it were days ago, so many things cannot have happened in so little time, and the exhaustion that overwhelms him is not only that of his body. It is simply too much—too much tragedy and emotion, too many decisions to be made, too many dead and too many gone away, more in one day than in his entire life, and his brain, his nerves have had enough: he feels a trembling in his hands, his head and chest burn with fever. His thoughts return to what Ambre said, part of him almost hopes they will be unearthed, unmasked, and everything will be over, because the waiting and uncertainty and fear—they are worse. But that is what Ambroisie-Father will be counting on if the Son's death is uncovered, the fear the peasants have of their masters: they will give themselves up, they cannot stand the terrifying dread of being caught. They would rather surrender, hurry to the slaughterhouse—and yet Eugène is not ready for that, nor is Ambre, let alone Germain and Mayeul, who have their lives ahead of them, lives with a future, perhaps, if fate is on their side, if they are lucky, if everything goes well. For Madelaine, there's no telling. Madelaine, who brought this upon them. Eugène shakes his head, he loves the girl. If everything goes as they hope, he will go and find her one day—that too perhaps, everything is uncertain, he imagines the smile on the girl's face, he'll set off on the road, he'll ask around, the big horse is something people notice, he'll bring them back. If all goes well, he tells himself again, in silence.

Germain and Mayeul scour the forest, rage in their hearts. One hand on the knife he has slipped under his coat, Germain dreams of killing anyone who gets in his way. Mayeul is silent, merely following his brother, he has to run to keep up. He knows that look of his. He heard the words, at the beginning, now Germain is silent. Germain has it in for the entire world for causing his life to collapse. For years he has been patiently constructing his apprenticeship, his vocation, his passion, stone upon stone, and all at once everything has gone to pieces; but his father could say the same, as could his mother. They have all lost, today. And Madelaine, the source of so much brokenness—the only one who might be able to put something right is the gray horse. So Germain leads Mayeul and runs silently through the darkness, covering twice as much territory as his parents, he hasn't asked himself what he'll do if he finds the horse. They didn't talk about it among themselves, Aelis just said they had to catch the creature before the soldiers did, there was little time, and off they ran. Bring him back to The Rises. And then. We'll see at that point, for the moment all his senses are turned to the sound of the horse, the smell of the horse, the idea of the horse, the horse is salvation, was what Aelis murmured, but the horse is nowhere to be seen.

Germain is the best mushroom picker in the village. He has an ability to stride through the woods and focus all his attention on the thing he is searching for. He no longer sees the leaves on the ground or the moss or the fallen branches, he no longer notices the old brown tree trunks, or the humus, or the places where the earth has been disturbed by a sleeping deer: only the mushrooms shine on his retina. He wanders through the forest and his gaze sweeps over the space on both sides at once, to his left and to his right, he feels his eyes getting bigger, his gaze splitting in two, each eye searching on its own side, on the alert for the hidden boletuses and chanterelles which suddenly appear deep in his pupil. He's doing the same thing now for the horse. He stops suddenly and, lowering his eyelids, draws a picture in his mind of the fugitive animal—the curve of its muscular back, its tangled mane falling onto its powerful neck, he envelops it in an animal smell of sweat and fear, then stares at it like that. Then he opens his eyes and he knows that nothing else will draw his gaze, that he can run through the woods now, he will not miss the gray horse. With Mayeul at his side, he continues his silent search in the direction of the farms.

But the Son's horse did not go as far away as they thought. Perhaps he had been trained to stay near the place where his master dismounted: when Madelaine's hatchet flew through the air and the horse bolted, terrified by the fury and the sound of breaking bones, it was to gallop into the forest, then very quickly he calmed down. With no rider to spur him on, he slowed to a trot, then a walk, stood still, head high, listening to what was behind him. Because he had put distance between himself and the danger, he began grazing. The bit disturbed him—but he's used to these solitary moments when Ambroisie-Son is dealing with a girl or a woman, or a wounded quarry, the horse has learned to eat despite the metal across his tongue, he has learned to wait.

So in the woods he waits. He wanders for hours, following the tufts of grass, sometimes stepping on his reins, which have slipped off and pull against his teeth. He drinks water from the stream, insects begin to hide for the night. The girth of the saddle is tight around his barrel, and he's used to that, too. At no time does he have the instinct or the desire to go back to the stable, he's eating his fill of tender grass, he has never been one for the herd, most of the time the Son goes around on his own and the horse is accustomed to the master's long outings where there are just the two of them and no one else. Only the hours passing strangely, without noise, without men, the freedom is disconcerting, and he drifts where the wind takes him, or a smell, or the random movement of his hooves. His senses are on the alert, the millennial instinct of his race, night and the unknown leave his nerves on edge; sometimes he breaks into a gallop for no reason, as if fleeing from an invisible danger, he snorts, hooves flying in the dark. But there, too, he stops before long, it's just a pretense, it's instinct, there is nothing in the woods.

Almost nothing.

And truth be told the horse is almost happy when he sees him all of a sudden. He recognizes the outline of a man, and it seems to him that everything is normal again. He gives a little whinny of welcome, the same he gives the stable boy who brings his oats morning and night, a coo a purr, he steps toward the figure then stops.

The man is a woman.

The horse is not afraid of women. There too, he is used to their smell, Ambroisie-Son often rides him to places where there are women. He doesn't like the sensations associated with those visits—the cries, the distress, the violence—but he has been trained to obey, he doesn't move, yet again he waits patiently. And this is what he does now: he waits for the woman in the woods to come closer, she is murmuring to reassure him, holds out her hand and takes the reins at his mouth.

Then he sees the shining knife hidden under her cape.

It is the same night and Madelaine is doing what Eugène told her to do: walking without stopping. The moon illuminates the towpath along the Basilic, where men have cleared the forest to leave room for the carts or oxen that sometimes pull the logs from the shore. Madelaine and Jéricho have fallen naturally into the same rhythm, their steps sure and slow, they both know that if they hurry they will tire before dawn. Madelaine doesn't speak, and the big horse, as he follows, looks at her small nervous figure, ordinarily so eager to talk. He is not used to walking at night. It doesn't bother him—he sees better in the dark than men do. It's a change. They didn't take the path to the ferry, and sometimes he turns his head to observe the paths back there that he is leaving behind, as the distance grows between himself and the stable where he ought to be. Madelaine's familiar presence reassures him. He breathes in her smell.

Madelaine holds the horse by the bridle. She too is gazing out at the night. It's been a long time since she rubbed up against it, the only memories she has of the night are those of abandonment, cold, and hunger, the fleeting refuge she found in empty huts, the solitude. But night is more than that, they say here that it is dangerous; when the day is waning, everyone goes home, men and animals alike, they leave room—they have no choice—for life in the wild, for thieves. Poachers venture out cautiously, you have to be used to the night, you have to have tamed it. As she reconnects with it, right from the start

Madelaine feels the force and calm of the black sky. She tells herself that there is nothing to fear from this awakening world, it is simply a different world, with other sounds, all she has to do is become familiar with them, she recognizes some of them, the furtive ruffle of a bird among the leaves, the squeak of a shrew. The air is cooler, Madelaine's cape keeps her in a cottony warmth. Because she is tired she closes her eyes, lets the horse guide her; it makes her feel a little dizzy, as if she were rolling down to the bottom of her body, and then to the bottom of the earth as it reverberates beneath her feet. She is anchored to something infinitely more vast than she is, she is the connection, a tiny connection between the sky and the earth and she occupies both territories, air and earth, head and feet. Sometimes she hears a faint melody, she knows it's inside, in her ears, it doesn't exist. She knows that it's the exhaustion but the sensation sweetens everything, she continues to move forward with the horse, she can hear his deep, regular breathing next to her, and then without warning it comes over her again.

The anger.

There is no more room for fear, and rage gives her cold sweats. At first, she hovered between apprehension and sorrow, numbed by an afternoon in May that suddenly became different. As the hours pass, the unease turns to fury. She contains it. She ruminates on it, endlessly repeating the gestures from earlier that day, she has no regrets; what she does regret is that it was she, Madelaine, who was forced to leave, when she is not guilty. Ambroisie-Son represents the absolute enemy, the evildoer, the one who wins no matter what. To be sure, he has not won outright—and Madelaine in her anger strikes the bound bag on the horse's back, she hears the dull sound it makes, as if the corpse had bumped against a tree. Oh, no, the Son has not won, look what he's come to, these bloody mortal remains are of no further use to anyone, but she, too, has lost everything, because of him, and that's what's unjust, that's what turns

Madelaine white with rage, makes her pound her fist against the bag, all she has left now is life. It's too little, too easy. A loathsome game, mere hogwash to be hushed: they would act as if nothing had happened. She wants no part of that lie, she's not cautious in that way. She doesn't have such confidence—everyone lied that day, and if you didn't lie it's because you're stupid, there is no happy medium.

It's not worth her hiding, given she's dragging this body with her. The Son raped and killed and this is his reward. He ruined their lives, creating absence, creating deception—Madelaine immediately understood that from that moment on, Ambre would pretend to be Aelis, Ambre her mother, she says, who has chosen Eugène over her, no matter how the girl tells herself that she understands, that maybe she would have done the same thing, it is still gut-wrenching, it does not console her. She has never confused the two sisters, she cannot get over the fact that Germain and Mayeul saw nothing, said nothing. She shakes her head—no, she doesn't confuse them. There's a scent, a vibration of the soul, when she stepped over that body with her hatchet, the moment Ambroisie-Son fell, she knew beyond the shadow of a doubt that it was Aelis there on the ground; Aelis whom they laid out in Léon's house to make believe that . . . And the girl knew it came to them all of a sudden, the look they gave each other, Eugène and Ambre, when they realized they could change things, that no one would notice, their only chance, their love.

Madelaine ruminates on this, too.

Love?

Love is a choice between rape and lies. And so it's always a sin, and again she hits the bag on Jéricho's flank, she hurls abuse, all this because of him, her voice resonating in the dark, it's as if there were ten Madelaines shouting, ten Madelaines swearing that they will hurt him, hurt him even more, that this is only the beginning.

Madelaine is shivering, there is fury, and there is the cold. This cold they feared for the sowing, she couldn't care less now, crops she'll never see growing, and again she adjusts the cape around her shoulders, her eyes raised to the sky stabbed with stars. The weather has changed yet again, a promise has slipped away, spring has evaded them, it's too late, she thinks, all the plants have already come up, they are fragile, frail, and the disaster is all the same to her.

Amid the darkness that is gradually lifting, Madelaine puts a hand on the reins to stop the big horse. This is the end of the forest, the countryside is opening out onto a plain where the grain has also sprouted, like at their farm. As dawn begins to break, chestnut trees, thirty years old or so, can be seen marking the border between wilderness and cultivated land, and Madelaine moves toward the trees. It will be here, yes, she thinks, on one of these young trees growing straight up to the sky, trees that will make perfect barrels someday—but for now she is not looking for lumber, she's looking for a post, a stake, a trunk on which to hang her fury. With a sharp movement she takes out her knife and severs the ropes holding Ambroisie-Son to the back of the horse, and the bag slides to the ground with a dull thud. Madelaine blows on her frozen hands. The wind has veered to the northeast, and this time, she's sure, the frost is on its way.

The very next day the icy air that everyone has been dreading freezes the young crops, burns the flowers on the fruit trees, shrivels the plants in the vegetable gardens. It crept in during the night, no one heard; the day before they'd told one another that it was getting chilly, and all the villagers thought about those bloody ice saints, but none of them imagined how extreme this wave of frost would be, lasting three days and four nights. Nature could not help herself. She let her flowers bloom, she thought she had the weather on her side. They should have lit fires the way they do in the wine country, to protect the crops; they should have covered their hectares with an impossible veil, should have spat in the air to warm it, and even so—nothing will save the young shoots from that wind that will not let up for almost four days, because it's the wind that is the most dangerous, the cold air passing in the sky, driving the temperature down by an entire season in a matter of hours, and once it has caught its prey it doesn't let go, all of Tuesday, of Wednesday, of Thursday.

By the dawn after the first night, they know. They will have to start over, at least where they can, and everything will be late, even if the season agrees to wait now, because the new seeds will need to catch up with the passage of time—and there aren't enough new seeds, they'll have to scrape the ground in their reserves and plant half-fields, and everyone is aware of what this means, given that they are indebted to the merchants as well—it will never end, they think, they are cornered.

But in fact it's a trifle, compared with what will soon befall them.

Within a few short days the inhabitants of La Foye have reorganized the entire survival of their year. The village is busy with farm workers driven by despair, and despair lends them unprecedented strength. In the most exposed fields where everything has burned, already the first morning they plow the furrows to prepare them for the new seeds. Eugène, Germain, and Mayeul have a plot of a few acres, and they dig up all the buckwheat that has already turned black. They say nothing about the absence of the big horse, which, if he were still there, might have saved them by helping to turn over the earth. In fact, they do not exchange a word that day, they're in a state of shock from the all too recent tragedy that they are trying hard to put to one side in their minds; they are almost glad of this frost, which keeps them busy and completely invests their souls, pushes Madelaine's departure into the background and with it the visceral fear of being caught.

They are all in the fields, young and old alike, so many ants scurrying about outside despite the wind that continues to freeze them, they are determined to plow the too-hard earth, but after the thaw every day will count, and they don't think about the implements that are vibrating through their bodies clear to their shoulders, and on to their heads, and the pain that keeps them from sleeping; they dig and delve and wield their barrow, they sweat despite the cold, death is licking at their hands. Once again there is that urgency to resist and, as always, they respond. They know in advance that not everyone will survive this new terrible year. And yet, as long as they're standing, they'll stake their all, they'll tear at their skin and break their backs, they'll wear themselves out, that's what they're made for.

But once again, nothing will be saved.

On the third day of the frost Ambroisie-Father's soldiers surround the village of La Foye. And not only La Foye: every hamlet, in the perimeter stretching from the château to the chestnut tree where the horribly mutilated body of the Son was found, is implicated.

When they laid before him the unrecognizable mortal remains of his heir, Ambroisie-Father turned pale. Because his Son is dead, yes—but above all, because of the way he died.

This was no accident. The brutality is unprecedented, staged in a way that has the Hinterland buzzing already in length and in breadth—Ambroisie-Son attached to a tree in broad daylight, exhibited for all to see, his entire torso split open with his guts spilling out and black blood splattered all over his face and body. An insane provocation, and all the peasants who hear the news freeze in terror despite their relief at knowing that the Son is dead. No master has ever been exterminated in this way. Masters die in battle, in duels, occasionally while hunting, and sometimes of illness. They're not massacred like paupers, they're not bled like pigs; and regarding this aspect, the execution leaves no doubt, it is the work of a pauper. Masters kill more elegantly, not with the aggression implied by such gaping wounds. Alas, masters do avenge their dead.

Thus the Son was found loosely strung to his tree, and soldiers have been crisscrossing the Hinterland in a mad rage. The same day, as they galloped along the Basilic, the troops stopped and noticed a strange mass in the mid-stream, caught in a tangle of branches. Two soldiers were dispatched into the water. They came back out pulling by the reins the body of Ambroisie-Son's gray horse, and beached it on the shore. The creature's carotid artery had been severed. From its swollen belly, they understand that the horse was killed at the same time as his master, and had the debris not trapped it there, the Basilic would have carried it to the edge of the territory, like a tree trunk left to the current. And there's something that doesn't make sense: such precautions taken to camouflage the horse's death, whereas the Son's body was fed to everyone's gaze, but this detail was swept aside by sorrow and shock, and then came Ambroisie-Father's explosion of rage. On a day of icy wind, the château shivers with hatred.

On the third evening of the frost, then, the soldiers charge into the village square. They come after the Angelus, when all the men are at home and all the houses have closed around them, and that is what the troops want: no one shall escape. There is no warning, and no explanation. What's more, the moment the armed men break down the doors of the first cottages and burst in, the peasants know why they have come, and what will ensue. It does not stop their cries, of the women and children, of the men, the moment the eldest son is dragged out of every house, the soldiers take them at random, the eldest children still at the supper table, the soldiers shove them, push them out onto the little square in the middle of the village. And in La Foye, as in the other hamlets, on the order of Ambroisie-Father the sons' throats are slit. There is no mercy and no salvation, the soldiers slash and their blades enter flesh. They work quickly, hardly looking, sometimes there are loud peals of laughter, they're warriors, death does not intimidate them. They leave a pile of bodies covered in blood, which their steaming horses crush underhoof as they gallop away. The petrified villagers watch as they make off toward the next village, the next place of eldest sons. The mothers' cries fill the sky.

At The Rises, the soldiers surround the farms, break down the doors to Eugène's and Léon's houses. They knock Eugène and Ambre senseless, ransack the two houses, all too empty. Leaning over Eugène, their swords demanding—but Eugène stammers that his sons are dead all, the others are dead too, there's no one left, and the soldiers search some more before they come back and lay into Eugène some more to take revenge on this sonless house, they beat him to a pulp, Eugène lies motionless on the red floor, the gallop of horses fades into the distance.

Later, when night has fallen, Germain and Mayeul come back from the fields. They had seen the soldiers running into the village, they heard them go up to The Rises. They hid. There was nothing they could do. They feel ashamed.

Ambre rushes to them, holds them tight, squeezes them, she thought they were dead. Joy is not spoken, precluded by fear and sorrow, but it is there, palpable, in the cries of the mother who is not the mother, they sob together. The sons are afraid the soldiers will come back; No, says Ambre, this time it's over. All of this, murmurs Germain, because of us—and Ambre puts a hand over his mouth, You must never say that again, not ever. You have to forget. Germain looks at his father, looks at his injuries, kneels down by him in silence. Eugène says he'll be all right. And then he smiles.

During the night, they hear sounds again, outside, and their hearts panic. They hide, as if they could disappear inside their walls, they avert their gaze, not to see if misfortune has returned. But the sound is regular, calm, insistent. It stops by the farm. It's Mayeul who recognizes it first, and he takes his hands from his face, leaps up, and before Eugène, terrified, can stop him, has the boy lost his mind, but Mayeul says, It's him, it's him, I know it is, I know it's him. As his parents and Germain look on, terrified, Mayeul opens the door. Jéricho is there.

After she had hung Ambroisie-Son's corpse from the chestnut tree, Madelaine set the big horse free. She turned him around, facing the place from where they had come, and with a slap on his rump she ordered him to go.

Go home.

Madelaine is getting rid of Jéricho. Because he'd be too visible in her flight if she has to hide for weeks, because they have far greater need of him back at The Rises than she does. Because he belongs to Eugène, and Eugène told her to come back in ten years' time. Come back to see him.

And her mother.

So they have to be there in ten years and the horse will be of more use to them than to her. In her mind, Madelaine draws a line tracing the first day of this immense time separating her from them. She looks down the road, standing there in the middle. For a moment she is tempted to turn back, to catch up with the big horse she just drove away. But all at once she turns in the direction that leads ahead of her and enters it, as if to escape.

At first light, when she pauses to look for a sheltered place to hide for the day, she stops by a bend in the river Basilic, goes down to the water, and takes out her hatchet. In the flickering reflection of the river, she cuts her hair short like a boy's. To make things perfectly clear to everyone: there is no fragility here. There is nothing female. She does not flinch when the first strands fall, and then the next. Nor does she flinch when after that she looks at her face in the water and sees this young boy with blue eyes, a boy who is too handsome, but life won't be the worse for it, she'll have to get used to it, she pulls the hood over her head because of the cold air on the back of her neck, and she slips into the hidey-hole she has found.

Time stretches to breaking point. It doesn't seem possible that the tragic event that cast her out on the roads was only yesterday, to her it seems like days, weeks ago, and the days and weeks to come will be years. Her perception is distorted, the paradox between the vivid images in memory, with the blood still boiling inside her, and the way she looks back at the drama from such a great distance that it cannot date from only yesterday, it has always existed—as if Ambroisie-Son had always been dead and in her mind Madelaine was observing the strange scene and her gaze was empty. She sleeps all morning from exhaustion. It's the long walk of the night and, above all, the emotion. On waking she will recall the unpleasant sensation of having lost the strength to get to her feet. Something is pinning her to the ground, closing her eyelids, taking her back into limbo, something soft and exhausted, and as she dozes off again she tells herself that it doesn't matter, only this tiredness matters, she slips into it with terrifying bliss. She hopes she can sleep for the rest of her life, let the bloodied mutilated bodies disappear; she hopes that she will awaken and laugh because it was all a dream and it is time to go with Germain to the fields now she's late, eventually she regains consciousness. She remembers everything, and everything is horribly real.

The day throws her off course with its immobility and silence. Madelaine is used to working for as long as the light allows, her body bent to the implements and the weight of the earth, she feels herself breathing, sweating, slowly standing straight again pressing her hands into the small of her back, and then: don't move, don't speak. Or else just quietly. And alone. She is puzzled to be sleeping during those hours when ordinarily she would be working her guts out, now this forced apathy, time too long, as if it were elastic. Night is late in coming, and with it her freedom regained, this itching for movement, too many things going round and round in her head. Sorrowful things, questions she has never had to ask herself about the next day, and the day after the next day, then all the days that follow: to do what, go where? For her, for them, the peasants, generations of families have been moored in the Hinterland, it is their only territory. Their roots go deep; when they speak about the village, they say *we*. We all. All of us. In an instant, everything known to her collapsed, Madelaine is holding emptiness in her hands and in her chest, where it pinches, where it hurts if you touch it. If someone asked her just then what she hopes for most of all in the world, she would say, to go back. To go back home. Home contains the country, gives it meaning, home is the country. And now—exile.

To walk for nights on end. At no time does Madelaine imagine the massacre that has taken place in the village, she does not know that the soldiers have completed their task, killed the eldest sons, or the sons they found, or that no one has been held to account, or that they are not following her. She does not know that it is pointless to run away, there are no hunters, no dogs, nothing. She could stop there but once again she does not know this, and so she keeps going for a long time, long after the frosts that burned the spring and left her shivering in the dark, long after the thaw that saw the peasants hastily replanting the last of the seeds they found, long after the rainy season which left them all drenched, and only then will she tell herself that she's gone far enough, that where she is now no one has ever heard of the Ambroisies, and she goes up to the biggest farm to ask for work, to do again for others what she will no longer be doing at home, not until ten years have gone by, she'll go home then, she thinks, she swears she will, and she starts to laugh.

About the Author

Born in Paris, Sandrine Collette divides her time between Nanterre, where she teaches philosophy and literature, and Burgundy, where she has a horse stud farm. She is the author of several novels, including *Nothing but Dust* (Europa, 2018) and *Just After the Wave* (Europa, 2020). *Madelaine Before the Dawn* was awarded the Prix Goncourt des Lycéens, the Prix Goncourt des Détenus, and the Choix Goncourt from Switzerland, Austria, Slovakia, Italy, Turkey, and the United States.